I0757428

WUSS
THE GIANT
SEA MONSTER
2ND EDITION

WUSS

THE GIANT SEA MONSTER

2ND EDITION

BRAD RENO AND CRYSTAL BROOK CONFRONT MOASM

G.G. ROYAL

Wuss The Giant Sea Monster 2nd Edition, Brad Reno and Crystal Brook Confront MOASM

This book is written to provide information and motivation to readers. Its purpose is not to render any type of psychological, legal, or professional advice of any kind. The content is the sole opinion and expression of the author, and not necessarily that of the publisher.

Copyright © 2021 by G.G. Royal.

All rights reserved. No part of this book may be reproduced, transmitted, or distributed in any form by any means, including, but not limited to, recording, photocopying, or taking screenshots of parts of the book, without prior written permission from the author or the publisher. Brief quotations for noncommercial purposes, such as book reviews, permitted by Fair Use of the U.S. Copyright Law, are allowed without written permissions, as long as such quotations do not cause damage to the book's commercial value. For permissions, write to the publisher, whose address is stated below.

Printed in the United States of America.

ISBN   978-1-955363-32-7   (Paperback)
ISBN   978-1-955363-33-4   (Digital)

Lettra Press books may be ordered through booksellers or by contacting:

Lettra Press LLC
30 N Gould St. Suite 4753
Sheridan, WY 82801
1 307-200-3414 | info@lettrapress.com
www.lettrapress.com

Wuss the Giant Sea Monster is packed with powerful emotional events and amazing action rescues! A real page-turner.

5 Stars J. Grahovac "Really like this author"

5 Stars R. Rojas "Love and a concerned relationship with emotions, excitement, and courage"

5 Stars Carmen Matos "Beautiful, Looking forward to more books by this author"

5 Stars Ramona M. "Thrilling and kept me on the edge through the whole thing. Hope the author continues the story."

Dedicated to my children.
They are my greatest treasure.

O Lord, how manifold are your works! In wisdom have you made them all; the earth is full of your creatures. Here is the sea, great and wide, which teems with creatures innumerable, living things both small and great. There go the ships, and Leviathan,* which you formed to play in it.

—Psalm 104:24–26

*Leviathan: It may describe a rare abomination of a species or one of many growing out in the deepest waters of the largest oceans of the world.

PART ONE

WUSS THE GIANT SEA MONSTER

In the great depths of the waters of Antarctica lives the colossal squid, *Mesonychoteuthis hamiltoni,* the largest and most aggressive carnivorous squid in the world, and it is capable of growing to lengths exceeding sixty feet. This great creature has only one mortal enemy, the largest mammal on earth, the sperm whale. The deep frigid waters of the South Pacific is where these prehistoric giants grow, and it is where these two giants, two of the largest creatures on earth, cross paths and battle for their lives against each other. Indisputable evidence, such as beaks of the giants, have been found in the stomachs of sperm whale carcasses. There is also evidence on whale skin that these beasts can cause grave damage to the whale as well. Razor-sharp hooks, some inches long, surround the suction cups that spread out down the monster's long snake-like arms by the hundreds. The evidence shows these deadly suction cups and hooks can attach; slice and rip apart large areas of a whale's skin.

Some have called the colossal squid the little brother of the Norse legend, the Kraken, but the Kraken was thought only to be a mythical beast. Now, this legend is thought to be more likely based on an actual sighting of a giant squid. The possibility of such a terrifying monster as this even existing for real instilled fear enough to keep many from ever venturing too far from shore. Stories have been told of monster sightings far out at sea by eyewitnesses. They are repeated by others and exaggerated and circulated around port cities and other places these sailors stop and tell their tales. The stories they tell seem incredible but somehow believable. Stories of sea monsters of such gigantic proportions seem impossible until described in fine detail by these eyewitnesses. Stories of the destruction of boats and cargo losses go back to the very earliest days of ocean exploration.

As the Viking legend attests, one of a monster so large, it was capable of wrapping its enormous tentacles completely around a passing ship and pulling it to the murky bottom of the deepest parts of the ocean. Eyewitnesses swore it was true, yet no carcass that large has ever been found. That would be definitive proof of the existence of a true Kraken. We already know that they live in the deepest parts of the world's oceans; perhaps they migrate back there to live out their life, so the legend lives on.

The home of this giant, the colossal squid, is in the deepest darkest waters of the oceans, hundreds and even thousands of feet down, as much as four miles deep into blackness. That is where these monsters live and should stay, but they do come to the surface for one thing—to feed. It has been suggested that their population is increasing. There are potentially thousands there of all sizes.

Like the vicious man-eating predators we know—lions, sharks, and alligators—these aggressive predators also stalk at night, swimming to the surface, searching for food, swimming swiftly with nothing to stop them. Like the pterodactyls of prehistoric times flying freely across the skies to search and pick their prey using their tremendous beaks and claws, the giant squid is a roaming terror of the seas.

The slightly smaller version, the Humboldt squids, are plentiful and have been seen working in unison using pack mentality to surround and attack their prey with lightning speed. With unexpected force, these squids ram their target at high-speed using the propulsion they generate by forcing water violently through their funnel. The blast from the funnel can launch the squids like missiles into its targets, and the blow can be crippling. These squids also have the ability to produce a thick inky substance to confuse their prey or enemy, whatever the case may be. They also have the ability to communicate with each other or disguise themselves to escape danger by changing the color of their skin. By contracting or expanding an elaborate system of pigment sacs called chromatophores, their colors change constantly as needed.

When they ram a target, they also use their tentacles to take bites of their prey at the same time. When they are ready to capture their prey, they spin their body around and display the most terrifying sight imaginable. From this perspective, it more closely resembles the bottom side of a live slithering bush hog about to grind up whatever it touches next with razor-sharp, hook-shaped jagged teeth circling suction cups along its snake-like arms, some reaching to ten, even to twenty feet long. At the center is a powerful beak, strong enough to smash bones to bits with ease. They wrap their vicious tentacles around their prey and carry their meal swiftly back to depths no ordinary creature could withstand.

In the deep abyss of the Sea of Cortez, near Baja California, lives a multitude of Humboldt squids with an average length of a full-grown one at approximately seven feet. Hundreds have been seen coming to the surface at night to devour unsuspecting prey. They can ram their target with what has been described by scientists as having the speed of a fast-pitched baseball, stunning, then grasping and holding their prey in a lethal grip. Nothing can match the savagery of these hunters, these night stalkers, predators at the top of their food chain, and with nothing to fear; they take what they want.

Like other predators, its motive is to find food, nothing more. There is no big agenda for these creatures that we know about. Their migratory habits are not understood, although these giants have been seen in various parts of the world's oceans. Science was unable to document their existence until recent years, so there has never been a documented human death from one but in this part of the ocean, the turbulent and unpredictable waters off the coast of Cape Horn, South America, in the waters near Antarctica, we know there have been plenty of shipwrecks here, so who knows? Things we do know: There is a large volume of deep water and the colossal squid, the largest carnivorous beast on earth, can grow to total lengths of over sixty feet due to abyssal gigantism at these depths. It's not known how many of these creatures are there, but we have now seen evidence in pictures and actual whale-size carcasses that have washed up on shore that they do exist and believe there are hundreds, maybe thousands with all sizes in-between, and their population is growing at an enormous rate. Two other things are also for certain: they come to the surface at night to feed, and when you're in the water with them, you are in grave danger.

WUSS: THE BIRTH

In the depths of the South Pacific, a mother colossal squid has stopped in her mission to find food in order to begin the process of ridding her enormous body of over ten pounds of larvae. Hundreds of these tiny squids, held together by a thick gelatin, are clumped together in a gigantic mass below her tentacles and are gradually released and carried away by the currents. Each one now appears as a fully formed squid called a chick, one quarter inch in length. Smaller fish start darting in to begin their feast, causing an increasing cascade of these larvae that catch the rays of sunlight from the surface and shimmer in the icy clear blue water. Any drifting downward still encumbered by the heavy viscous gel glimmer like diamonds as they rain down into darkness. With sunlight streaming on beams of light, near-microscopic life becomes visible. The many squids find nourishment immediately, while many more begin to break loose and drift away individually, being carried at the tide's mercy.

In the most unlikely of events, the shimmering reflective light of the drifting squid larvae catches the attention of a sperm whale passing by along the South American coastline. The whale decides to make a meal of this squid and turns to attack. Now is one of the only times whales will use their tremendous speed and weight to attack with ferocity in an effort to kill another animal nearly as large as himself.

The squid is unable to prepare and starts to flee. Baby squids, known as chicks, scatter and drift like snowflakes; as she moves gracefully trying to elude the largest animal on earth. The whale slams into the giant squid only to find his head being grasped, carved, and sliced by this aggressive adversary. The whale clamps down hard on the mantle of the monster even as gashes are being ripped everywhere the vicious razor-sharp circular ridges catch hold and suction cups stick to the thick whale skin. The remaining larvae are swept away. The whale, being unable to continue the fight, turns his body toward the ocean floor to smash the giant against the hard rocky surface and put an end to the torture he was enduring. In the end, the whale, with the enormous carcass in his grasp and with extremely long tentacles drifting alongside him, continues on his way into the darkness.

Quiet returns to the ocean as the currents return to their normal conditions. Many of the squids drift downward, a few are carried further. Sea life is plentiful in this part of the ocean. One small squid was swept up in unusual sea currents created from an El Niño weather pattern and unusual timing. The shift in the currents carried the young giant north of Peru. The ocean currents, along with atmospheric conditions, had caught hold of the rarely seen creature and had carried him into the stronger currents of the South Pacific, further north past Columbia, and into the waters off the coast of Central America. As the currents carried him north, food became more and more plentiful, and he began to grow.

Now, with the body the size of an ear of corn and with tentacles easily twice as long as his body, he is swept up in the undertow of a passing ship as it enters the Panama Canal. With each stage of the process, the monster freighter makes its way slowly through the canal with the younger monster being swept alongside for the ride. The strong current pulled the small squid alongside the black behemoth, and like a baby, the young giant followed the freighter close as if he were following his mother.

Once through the Panama Canal, he was carried north by the Gulf Stream into the rich warm waters of the Gulf of Mexico. About twenty miles off the coast of Florida due west of St. Petersburg, he found a home. In an area where the water was only about sixty feet deep, he happened upon a drop-off. Dropping nearly a hundred more feet to the bottom, he began to descend into the depths. Here his food was plentiful, and the waters were dark and cool. He doesn't think of where he is or how he got here. He doesn't think of going back to where he came from because he doesn't look back. He is a hunter, a predator.

With his food supply plentiful and no competitors, he began to grow, and by the end of his third month in the gulf, he was passing six feet; three months later, ten. He continued to thrive, never encountering any human, rising to the surface at night to search for sources of larger prey as he grew. He stayed low in the cool darkness of the depths during daylight hours, and by the end of his first year, he was twenty-five feet long and weighed over three hundred pounds. His appetite was increasing, and his hunting ground for food was becoming less adequate in supplying his daily requirements. His mantle was over ten feet long, and his eight arms and two longer tentacles added fifteen to twenty more feet to his total length. His needs outweighed his available food source now, so he stayed hungry most of the time.

+Wuss the Giant Sea Monster

CHAPTER 1

SATURDAY MEMORIAL DAY WEEKEND

May 27

Brad Reno was lying on his cot below the deck of his 22-foot fishing boat listening to the waters splash against its sides, thinking about the events of the day while his fiancé, Candy Cotton was still up on the deck. Brad wasn't content in his thoughts. His heart was breaking knowing what it was he had to do. The waters were calm and it was close to dusk when he stopped the boat for the night in the Gulf of Mexico about 20 miles west of St. Petersburg, Florida. He had a lot on his mind as he lay there thinking of the events of the past two days and his head began swirling. He had to make up his mind about what he was going to do about Candy. He had decisions to make involving many different things. What was he going to say, and how and when was he going to say it. He loved Candy so much but he couldn't take the cheating anymore and when she drank too much, she lost all control and would do the most disgusting and deceitful things one could do in a relationship. He still loved her, though. He lay on the cot not knowing how he was going to tell her goodbye. Even though it has been a long time coming, it was the events of two days ago that weighed heavy on his heart now enough to know that their relationship had to end.

As Brad lay there trying to relax, he was unaware that 150 feet beneath his boat in these murky, tepid waters precisely where he stopped lurked something unimaginable, maybe even prehistoric, and it slowly began to rise to the surface. It hadn't eaten much lately and was starving, and the search for food is the only reason it ever comes to the surface. This creature was enormous but at the same time, it was elusive. It moved quietly and quickly when it needed to. It didn't like to be seen. It lived in the deepest, darkest waters in the ocean but now it was here directly under his small boat, moving and spreading out its enormous deadly tentacles, over 20 feet long, gracefully but eerily around as it slowly ascended barely disturbing the water in its search for food.

Brad tried to put his problems with Candy out of his mind for right now and to think of less troubling things. Like today, while skimming along the wave tops, looking out over the vast ocean waters of the gulf, he was reminded of his Navy days back in his youth. He had been stationed at Camp Lejeune, North Carolina with the 2nd Marine Division as a hospital corpsman in the Fleet Marine Force. While there he trained along-side the marines and learned skills he's used plenty since then including scuba diving, which he did for fun now and rappelling from helicopters which he hasn't done since, but it was all part of his training. Remembering his friends from those days was a nice respite from the decisions he was about to make.

Brad was becoming sleepy as he felt the boat's movement on the ocean's surface. He recalled how much he loved the ocean as a kid and never passed up an opportunity to go to the beach and take a swim in those days. Since then, he has scuba dived off the coasts of Florida and North Carolina, the Hawaiian coast and the Pacific Ocean west of Mexico, exploring coral reefs and observing the sea life. He and a group of shipmates even went on a shipwreck dive while on leave in the Caribbean. They all loved the ocean so much back then and he was glad to have those good memories. He still kept in touch with a few friends from those glory years and wondered what happened to others.

His mind was busy as his thoughts turned to dreams and drifted back to his college days. He met Connie there and fell in love. He remembered the campus and her beautiful smile as they anxiously met between classes to spend every minute they could together. They graduated together and were married. It wasn't long before they had a beautiful daughter, Dee. He thought of Dee tonight and worried about her, too.

He took his business degree and began working in the pharmaceutical industry. He regretted that his marriage hadn't worked out, but he was able to spend more time with his grown daughter now. As he thought of those he loved, his dreams turned back to Candy. Suddenly, the creature below became aware of something floating on the surface. It moved faster now but still graceful and with ease as it quietly reached the surface and began to encircle the boat. That's when Brad felt a slap against the outside wall of the bulkhead where he was lying and it startled him awake. Then he heard Candy call his name, "Brad, come here! You got to see this!"

WUSS THE GIANT SEA MONSTER

2 days earlier - May 25

The ringtone from his fiancé's cell phone lying on the bedside table next to him started playing its familiar incoming text tone. He looked at the clock. It was 6:30 a.m., and Candy was up already and in the shower; he heard the water running in the master bath. He reached for the phone and saw just the last part of the message across the top of the screen before it went to saved messages. It said, "I had a dream about you last night," and then was gone. He wasn't expecting that and just lay there feeling pale and weak-kneed without even moving, letting what he just read soak in. He was afraid to move or try to get up; afraid he might not make it.

Who was *that* on the phone? He must know her pretty well to be texting her messages like that. He lay back, closed his eyes, and started thinking back. She went to visit her mom last weekend. He knew her mom. Did she see someone there? He had no reason to suspect anything; they were very close. The only recent night she went out without him was last Wednesday when she met her former boss and now girlfriend for dinner to catch up on gossip. They were best friends and talked a lot, both 10s, and even though Joy was older than Candy by ten years, she had an elegant grace and narrow hips that caused men and women to do a double-take the closer they got to her.

Candy was in her forties with blond hair and a great body with a nice full figure; and she didn't have any dresses that weren't miniskirt length. Her legs were athletic but not muscle bound; sexy beautiful would be a better way to describe them. She attracted the attention of men looking for female company in the bar scene. Her body released these totally intoxicating pheromones that caused men to try to move in on her, sometimes even while he was sitting there. Boy, would he get angry. It would kill the evening for him, and he would be ready to go but not Candy; she would be ready for another drink. He had completely decided she was the classic example of a binge drinker. After a few drinks, she would become more playful; four or five, she might try to stand up on the table. She didn't get full or sick, just drunker, and she would just keep drinking. So far, he's been able to keep her from climbing up on the bar when she was with him, but she has tried, and the thongs she wears don't cover much. After eight to ten drinks, she would move onto the dance floor and sometimes get overly friendly to men, the taller the better. She liked reaching up and putting her arms around their neck. Sometimes she would turn around from him and start dancing with someone else or give some other guy she thought was cute a flirty look or tight hug, and that really blew his mind. He remembered many times feeling like he was going to have to fight his way out of some of these places.

Today was a different sort of trip, and he hoped she would find some joy in it. He loved her and wanted her to be closer to him, and he wanted her to convince him that she did love him, but so far, it wasn't looking good. She came out of the bathroom with one towel wrapped around her from under her arms down to miniskirt length. She was twisting her long blond hair in another one.

Brad had turned back over to face the wall like he hadn't looked at the phone. "Your phone went off," he said while trying to sound sleepy, but all the moisture was gone from his mouth.

"It did?" she answered back. "Probably Mama." She picked up the phone, unlocked it, turned around, and left the room without saying anything. He was sure that he saw her starting to smile as she looked down at her phone and closed the door, still wearing only a towel around her body and one around her hair. This was not the first time she had given him cause for concern. He started remembering another incident when they had been out and she got drunk and then she got mad when he tried to take her home and wasn't ready to go.

She wanted him to leave her there, just leave her there and go home. Things nearly got really ugly when some guy thought she needed protection from him. For a few seconds, he wasn't sure she was going to leave with him. Thank goodness the guy backed off when he told him she had too much to drink and he was taking her home.

That was only about three months ago; he

remembered the day because it scared him to death. They were leaving for Sanibel Island, Florida, today for a few days in the sun. He was looking forward to a little sightseeing time at the beach and a day of fishing. That's what he was hoping anyway, but images of the text message kept running like a jet printer across his mind's eye. His feelings of being rejected and replaced by some jerk she met in a bar were starting to consume his thoughts. He hoped there was nothing to it and he didn't want to bring it up if there was nothing to it, but if there was, he wanted to know.

"Come on! Get up if we're going!" Candy called from the hallway. She didn't have her phone with her when she came back into the bedroom, and she wasn't smiling now.

CHAPTER 2

On the way to Sanibel Island, he tried to observe her type her security number in her cell phone without being noticed. He had caught the first three numbers earlier—2, 2, 6—now she was picking up her phone and typing again. He waited until she typed a couple of numbers and then glanced her way while she focused on the keypad and got the rest—3, 9, 3.

She looked at him, smiled, and said, "You excited? You don't look very excited to be going this morning. Last night you were in a great mood."

"I'm excited. It'll be fun," he managed to say. To change the subject, he added, "Are you hungry? It's lunchtime."

They pulled off the highway into a touristy-looking upscale shopping area. He found a place to park, and they went into a trendy cafe that just opened for the day and found a table.

A waiter approached them. "Can I get you

something from the bar?" he asked, looking at Candy. "I'll have a glass of white wine, please," she answered.

"I'll have a Corona Light," Brad said when the waiter looked his way. "Are you ready to order?" he added.

"Give us a few minutes." Candy smiled at him as he turned to go. "I'm going to the bathroom," she said, then got up, leaving her purse and phone right there and just taking her makeup bag.

He picked up the phone, quickly typed in the code as he began to feel flushed. He started shaking and could barely press the buttons. Then he saw the unfamiliar name: Omar. He clicked on it, and sure enough, that was it. A stream of messages starting last Thursday and now leading to conversations like this. He was curious about what Candy said in reply to his confession of dreaming about her.

He found the message: "I had a dream about you last night." His heart was pounding; he felt like he just had three cups of coffee. Her response was what had him nervous as he scrolled down to read what she had written. It was clearly not what he was hoping, that she would excoriate him for sending her such a message. That she was in love with someone else and he should not text her anymore. That's what he hoped, but that's not what he read.

"Tell me about this dream," she replied. "I'd rather show you," he finished.

His heart sank as the sound of a cold wet bottle of Corona Light being set on the wooden table broke his focus on the phone. He realized he had slumped over and straightened up in his seat a little. A glass of wine for Candy was set across from him. He looked at the waiter, who was looking at him, and Brad said thank you. He knew he wasn't smiling, but he didn't care. He felt like his face was flushed too.

"Would you like an appetizer or something else?" the waiter asked. He thought for a second. "Would you bring me another?"

The waiter nodded, turned, and walked back to the bar area. He picked up the ice-cold beer and started guzzling it. Nearly half the beer was gone from the bottle before he set it down. It didn't help; his hands were still shaking. He felt weak all over like all the blood was draining from his body along with the love in his heart; it was melting and dripping out until it's all gone. The one woman he once described as the woman of his dreams is now in someone else's dreams. He had a nightmare of his own last night where he was sitting at a table with her at a nightclub and this guy came to the table to ask her to dance. Brad told the intruder if she wanted to dance, he'd dance with her himself. Then she got up anyway and started dancing with him. It wasn't long before his hands started wandering down to her beautiful ass, and she just kept dancing and smiling. That's when, in his dream, he got up to cut in. Candy looked at him like he was interrupting something she was enjoying very much and said, "If you don't go sit down, I'm going to call the police right now!" Then in his dream, she pulled out her phone and pressed 9.

Brad couldn't take any more. He took another drink of his beer. How could she do this? She hadn't had her engagement ring six months. How much money has he spent on her? He knew they had gone to Atlanta alone over ten times, twice to NYC, and three trips to Orlando. Trips to Helen, Georgia, in the summer, DC and Virginia for skiing in February and visiting vineyards for taste-testing wines in the summer. They had even planned to go on a cruise in a few weeks, and the ring was expensive, from the most prestigious jeweler in town.

He sat down feeling a lump grow in his throat as he began to decide what to do. He looked up, and with no sign of Candy, he grabbed his phone and snapped pictures of her conversation with Omar and his phone number so she couldn't deny it when he did ask her about it. He then put her phone back in her purse and picked up his beer for another big gulp just as Candy came back to the table.

She sat down and picked up the menu. The waiter came back and set the second Corona Light on the table, then asked, "Have you decided what you're having?"

"Yes, I'm getting the salad with grilled shrimp," answered Brad.

"Okay, and you, ma'am?"

"That sounds good. I'm hungry," she continued saying, "I think I'll have the prime rib, medium rare with a salad and ranch dressing and baked potato."

The waiter finished getting the order, and Candy asked him about the place, "What kind of place is this?

Do you have live music?" she asked, while looking around at the small stage with show posters and announcements on the walls.

"Yes," he said, "we have live bands in the evenings. Are you going to be around here this evening? This band comes in at nine with a great show, and last time they were here, the lead singer was a woman that wore an entire one-piece jumpsuit outfit made from flesh-toned nylon. It looked entirely like she was naked." Candy's mouth dropped open. "It was so funny when she would walk up to men with their dates," he finished.

"I'll bet," Brad added.

The waiter stopped looking at Candy finally, turned toward him, and said, "I'll go put your order in," and walked away.

He wasn't sure how to get this conversation started. He decided he needed more time to think about how to approach the subject.

CHAPTER 3

During the drive, she continued the odd behavior, snapping selfies and maybe even sending them out, he wasn't sure.

"Let me see your picture," he said.

"You pay attention to the road," she snapped back and went ahead texting and occasionally smiling.

No point in him asking her who she's talking to; he really didn't think she would be truthful, and she would probably get mad if he asked. Probably Omar anyway, maybe he should just ask her right now if that's Omar she's texting. Of course, with his luck, it would be the one time when she was texting her mother. How could she do this? How in the world could he love this woman so much? He wanted to cry right then and there, but he just stared at the road ahead without saying anything.

They pulled into the condo parking lot and began carrying stuff in planning to spend Memorial Day weekend here. He bought the condo late last fall, and it came with a boat slip; he didn't have a boat to put into his boat slip, so he bought one. His twenty-five-foot Boston Whaler, with the twin 120 HP Mercury engines, was there waiting at the dock, serviced and ready to go.

He had been waiting for this moment since he got it late last year. He puttered around along the coast a few times during the winter, but now it's warm enough to go further out, so this time they were going to spend a night out to see what it was like. He had been looking forward to fooling around with her on the boat too, but he wasn't sure now. There was some cold distance here, and she hasn't said much this trip either. Maybe she's infatuated with Omar.

Later they went out for dinner to a local seafood restaurant. She had a great-looking seafood platter with perfectly fried scallops, shrimps, oysters, and a fillet, to drink, a margarita with Jose Cuervo tequila. He had the blackened grouper with a Corona Light. Food was one thing they could agree on, and they ate out plenty, and the drinks kept coming. After dinner, Brad drove to the beach to take a walk with her there; she seemed to enjoy it too. On the way back to the condo, they saw a little night club with the bass beat reaching the highway and stopped for a drink. She wanted a Cosmo; he had a Corona Light. She drank that one down before the waiter came back and said she wanted another one. After a while, she started looking around, didn't see the waiter, so she got up and went to the bar. There wasn't but one empty place at the bar and that's where she stood, swaying her hips to the beat of the music.

Eyes followed her hips and legs moving beneath

the miniskirt. Her steps were measured and careless as she was starting to feel the effects of the booze. She was getting louder and bumped into a guy on the way back who looked at her and said, "What the f—, lady. You nearly made me spill my drink."

She stopped, looked at him, smiled, and motioned with her finger to come closer. She grabbed his chin, pulled him down, and kissed him right on the lips. Then she said, "I'm sorry," and came back to my table. "Don't you want another drink?" she asked.

Brad looked toward the guy she kissed; he was looking back. His only thought now was that it was time to go. She was finishing off her drink, standing by the table, moving her hips to the loud music. Then she put her hands on the table like she was going to climb on top of it to dance. Brad reached to hold her hand, but she snatched it back.

"You weren't going to climb on the table, were you?"

She gave him a not nice look, sat down, and said, "I want another drink!" more loudly. She abruptly stood up and ran smack into this young black guy.

Trying to be diplomatic, Brad said excuse us to him, and to her, he said, "We've got a big day planned for tomorrow, let's get the check and go." He reached for her hand, but she snatched it away again.

Then the young guy came back up behind her, grabbed hold of her other hand, and started pulling her away with him toward the other side of the room. She was being pulled away by a stranger! Brad thought it was incredible that she would be so careless. She wasn't even looking at the guy who had hold of her! She was looking at him! She was angry with him for not leaving her alone!

Brad caught up to her and grabbed her hand again. The guy yelled, "Turn her loose!" "No! She's with me!" Brad yelled back and held tightly to her hand and told *him* to turn loose. Then a bouncer walked up, and the young guy walked away. The bouncer took one look at Candy and said, "You need to leave." She then proceeded to tell him that she wasn't ready to leave. He led them both to the door anyway and watched them walk out. Candy was still being belligerent and wanted to go back in while Brad kept trying to coax her to come with him. They made it outside, but then she proceeded to walk around to another entrance.

"Candy? What are you doing? They told us to leave."

There was another bouncer at that door. He had been warned about her and stopped her from entering. Brad put his hand on her shoulder to get her attention away from the bouncer, but she slapped his hand away hard and said, "Don't touch me!" Then she turned toward Brad, looked coldly and directly into his eyes with pure anger, and slapped him sharply rapid fire, left, right, left, right, against both cheeks with both hands without saying another word.

The bouncer saw this and said, "I'm going to call a policeman if you don't leave now, there's one right out front!" She looked at him angrily and turned away reluctantly to leave with Brad. No words were spoken during the ride back to the condo. Brad looked her way only once; she appeared to be asleep. When they made it back to the condo, Candy fell into bed still half dressed.

Brad looked at her and asked, "Are you okay?"

"I'm fine!" she said, as she looked at him with her lazy-eyed sexy look she has when she's had too much to drink. Then she got up, went to the bathroom, put on a nightie, and came back to bed and turned toward him. That was their signal, and he lay down beside her and began gently kissing her.

"Wait," she said and sat up, pulled the nightie off back over her head, and cuddled up to him. Her scent was intoxicating, and he was totally infatuated with her.

CHAPTER 4

The morning came too early. They finally did wake up and started moving slowly getting ready for their first overnight boat trip. After eleven, they left the condo to get breakfast at a diner a couple blocks away. A lot of tourists were around, but they finally got a table, and the waitress poured their coffee.

Candy also ordered a Bloody Mary with vodka. Brad wanted to talk to her about last night, but he didn't want to start an argument.

"Do you remember anything about last night?" he started the conversation.

"I had a good time. Didn't you have a good time?"

Without hesitation, Brad seized the opening. "No, it was one of the worst, most harrowing experiences of my life." The couple at the next table looked their way. "You could have gotten us both hurt or arrested last night. You nearly let a stranger drag you out of the place while you were trying to get away from me." Brad realized he said that a bit too loud and lowered his tone.

"I did not!" she snapped back. She was starting to get riled.

Brad knew he should have stopped there, but no, not him. "I could have lost you. If that guy who grabbed you hadn't been alone, two together might have managed to get you out of there. He could have put you in a van, shot you full of heroin, and you'd be doing tricks on the street by this afternoon. You're an alcoholic." He finally stopped talking, but it was too late, her tolerance of his ranting became too much to take.

"You're crazy! I had too much to drink last night and I got drunk! I am not an alcoholic," she stated even louder back.

The waiter brought their meals and looked at her glass. "Another Bloody Mary, ma'am?" she asked.

"Yes, thank you," Candy replied, smiling politely up at the server.

The rest of the meal was eaten in silence. He paid the bill, and they left the restaurant and went back to the condo for the few things they had readied earlier. Brad added ice to the ice chest and started packing sodas. Candy liked Summer Time Lemonade drinks in twelve-ounce cans, so he bought a case. He also packed 16 oz bottles of water, a case of Diet Cokes, a case of Corona Lights, a case of Ultra Lights for Candy, and three bottles of white wine and a bottle of red. Then they packed bread, sandwich meats, and condiment essentials just in case they didn't catch anything. For dinner tonight, he planned to grill a couple of steaks on a small gas grill. He had also brought a bag of salad with a bottle of ranch dressing and a bottle of Sirah to go along with his planned romantic dinner under the stars. He loaded everything onto a cart and wheeled it down to the dock and to his boat that was moored there in its slip looking ready to go.

It was a beautiful day of blue skies and calm seas. A warm breeze and squawking seagulls flying around calling to each other appeared to be enjoying the day as well. They stopped at the office to tell John, the manager of the place, their plans for an overnight trip. He assured Brad he would notify the Coast Guard station of their trip and he would be there tomorrow when they got back. "Great," Brad said. "You're gassed up and ready to go. You have extra gas stowed in containers if you need it, but you shouldn't," he said confidently. "Ice in the fish well too," he added. "An optimist," Brad said back, then he thanked him. "Okay," and he turned his attention toward Candy. "Can you think of anything else we might need?"

"No, let's go. I'm ready to get going," she said, looking a little irritated.

Brad looked at the manager. "Do you by any chance know how far cell phone service reaches out?" he asked John.

"About twenty miles, I'd guess. It varies, some folks say their phones work until the battery dies." "Yes, that sounds about right . . . Well, good," Brad smiled, nodded goodbye, and headed toward the door.

Candy returned to the cash register with a Coke and medium-sized bag of pork skins while he ran back up to the condo and came back with his beautiful Yamaha guitar. He didn't play it much anymore, but he did have a song he had written that he began thinking about back on Valentine's Day, so he named it, "My Valentine's Song." He wanted to sing it to her if he got a chance; it helped his singing to have his guitar accompaniment, plus, she liked him to play "Home" by Philip Phillips.

Within the hour, they had gone about seven or eight miles out. Brad baited up the lines, and they started trolling for tarpon. Trolling along, the lines set, Candy was sitting between the two rods facing the trail of water behind sipping on a glass of Chardonnay with her eyes closed dreaming she was somewhere else, and Brad was at the helm staring at her from behind. He was mesmerized by her beauty, and no matter what her behavior was, he couldn't take his eyes off her when she was near and he could always smell her. He would take in deep slow breaths to take in as much as he could of her musky feminine odor. She was wearing her Colorado Rockies hat. He bought her that hat because it had the big CR logo on the front, and those would be her initials once they were married. He remembered buying it at the airport in Atlanta.

Today she was wearing a pink bikini with the top loosely tied in the back, revealing her shapely breasts and her beautifully defined legs with the sexiest ass he ever saw. A little muscular, but that made her butt a little fuller and rounder. When she wore short shorts or cutoffs, he couldn't leave her alone. He was cruising along with the rhythm of the waves trying not to bounce their teeth out, enjoying the view.

The ride so far had been nice too. *Wheeeezzz* went the line on the right-hand reel. Candy sat up with her wine glass still in her hand, watching the line being pulled out of the reel fast enough to burn your fingers if you tried to stop it. The ride had been quiet up until now.

"Set your glass down, Candy! You got a fish to catch," Brad yelled. He slowed the boat to idle, grabbed the other reel, and quickly began to get it out of Candy's way. She sat her glass down in the cup holder and picked up the reel. The line had stopped going out. "Reel!" Brad instructed her. She started reeling in the slack. "Faster, Candy! Reel it faster!"

"I am!" she yelled back, grinning big. All of a sudden, the line became taut again and disappeared under the boat. The drag released the line with another *wheeeeezzz*. This time the line went straight down. It had strength that gave the impression that this fish or whatever could easily break this line.

Candy stayed in her seat and held on as the rod bent to a perfect C shape toward the water as she reeled and pulled and reeled some more. Her face had a determined smirk on it. Then without warning, the line straightened out again. She stopped reeling to see what was going to happen next. At that moment, the line tightened with a jerk, then the downward motion stopped. Candy started reeling in some line, and in the middle of a turn, the line sprung tight and snapped. The boat that had been tipped by the weight of the fish, bobbed back up into the wave tops, and briefly caused them both to have to catch themselves. Now the boat rode the waves more easily without the weight of this fish or whatever on it. They would never know for sure what it was she had been fighting with for almost ten minutes because it was long gone.

Brad looked at her, she looked at him, and at first, they started smiling, and then they both just burst out laughing and started recanting the experience they just had.

"Did you see it?" Candy asked excitedly.

"I saw it dragging the boat around for ten minutes!" Brad said. "You should have seen your face. Your tongue was hanging out."

They both burst out laughing again. "Take a break," and he handed her a beer.

"Whew! I didn't realize how much work that was going to be!" she said, still excited and wearing the biggest smile he ever saw.

"Is that why you're grinning so big?"

Then she looked at him seriously and nodded her head slowly before they broke out laughing again. They were starting to have a good time.

"Are you hungry?" he asked.

"Yes," she acknowledged, and they went to the galley to start cooking the steaks they brought. They made love under the stars that night after all. "Who would have guessed it," he said out loud. "Guessed what?" she asked.

"Candy?" he asked.

"What?" she answered.

"I love you," he said, but he felt so sad.

"I love you too," she said back.

He felt a twinge above his left eye like a soft but unexpected slap that caused him to furrow his brow some. She got up and went to the cot inside the small cabin to sleep while he sat out a while. He was so brokenhearted. He still loved her deeply and dearly, and with every breath, he would gladly tell anyone who asked, "Yes! I love her," but he was pretty certain that he could never trust her again. He couldn't live like this, and he knew it. He went to the other cot and lay down. He could hear Candy's breathing, slowly and deeply. He was always impressed with how easily she fell asleep.

CHAPTER 5

The noise was surprising. Being startled awake by something slapping the side of the boat out here was strange. Candy wasn't beside him, so he thought it must have been her.

"Brad! Come here!" he heard her calling him from the bridge. Suddenly an even louder slap struck the boat and then another just outside of the bulkhead he was standing beside. Brad made his way out onto the deck. Candy was standing toward the bow in front of the windshield on the port side pointing out to sea.

Brad heard himself say, "Wow!" He didn't know why such a large quantity of fish would be doing this all at once. He stood there wishing he had a better camera than the one on his phone to catch this. He felt like what they were witnessing was nothing short of astonishing, as his eyes adjusted to the darkness lit only by the bright moon and its reflection off the water on this cloudy night. Waters showed only small white-capped waves, mostly calm except for the fish leaping and zigzagging away, and then on the other side of them, he saw countless numbers of medium to small fish leaping out of the water in an uncontrolled fashion. They weren't running together in a school like fish do, but scattered and chaotic, jumping in all directions.

Then a large wave of water rolled under them, and something hard bumped the bottom of the boat, lifting them above the waters around them and then easing them back down. The fish, suddenly as they began, stopped jumping. Not one more fish jumped.

"That was eerie," Brad said. "What was that?" Candy asked.

"I have no clue. Looked like something was chasing them, maybe a dolphin or something. It's gone now," Brad said.

"It lifted up the boat." Candy said back seriously.

Brad looked at her, absorbing the meaning of what she said but believing any danger was long gone, and asked her to come back to bed.

"I will in a few minutes," she said; then she grabbed her windbreaker to shield her from the cooling breeze, wrapped it around her shoulders, and sat down in her recliner.

He saw her shiver before he turned to go back to bed. No sooner was he starting to drift off than he heard her calling him again, "Brad, come here, quick!" He heard an occasional fish hitting the boat: "Look, they're doing it again!"

For a moment in the darkness, he thought that it might be raining, but if it was, it was raining fish. Candy was standing on the bow, watching the fish activity by the light of the full moon. Suddenly and with nothing visible in sight, the boat was bumped hard and began rocking violently. Candy screamed and Brad looked up in time to see a monstrous slimy arm larger in diameter than a full-grown anaconda come across the bow and sweep Candy overboard. There was nothing he could do. It was over.

"Candy!" He ran to the bow where she was just standing and looked into the waters that were starting to calm. Only a few fish were still jumping now; everything grew quiet. He started shaking violently as he was looking all around as far as he could see. He was ready to jump in. He had grabbed the round life preserver as he ran toward where she went in. He was prepared to jump in, but when he got to the edge and looked for her, he didn't see her or any sign of her anywhere. There was no splash or scream, nothing. He was ready to jump; he wanted to jump, but where was she?

"Candy!" he screamed. He cupped his hands around his mouth and yelled at the sea, "Candy! Candy! Candy!" He ran on the other side of the boat but saw nothing there either. He noticed all the fish had all stopped jumping. He stood there scanning the ocean for any sign and climbed as high as he could on the deck and called her name as tears rolled down his cheeks.

"Oh my god," he cried, "what's happened?" Then he turned his head toward the sky and yelled, "God? What was that?!" He finally sat down on the deck. He was thinking about everything, and his mind was racing. He started thinking about Candy. "It all came down to love, didn't it?" Why would he be thinking that now? He remembered part of scripture in one of the New Testament books that described what love is. "Love is kind, love is patience," he forgot the rest right now. Maybe it would come back to him. It was good. He shook his head up and down. "It was good," he said, talking to himself out loud now, he remembered that much. Why is he thinking that? Was he in shock?

Suddenly he thought about her family. "I have to tell her mother and brother. Oh my god!" He thought about it for a second, then it hit him, and his bottom jaw dropped open. "What am I going to tell them?" A sob burst from his throat. He started thinking out loud. "I can't tell them that a giant octopus grabbed her off the boat! Who in the hell would believe that? Oh my god! What can I say?" His face was contorted by the weight of anguish he felt inside. His ache was so debilitating he couldn't seem to move. He just sat there and cried out loud, "Oh my god! I hope no one thinks I would hurt her! Oh my god! Oh my god!"

Sweat rolled down his face mixing with tears, he cried, "What can I say? How can I explain this so that reasonable people will believe it? They are *not* going to believe it, is what they are going to think. No one is going to believe that an octopus large enough to grab someone off a boat this big with his giant arm even exists!" Then he thought, "Maybe I was wrong, maybe it was a shark or a killer whale," as his mind raced trying to find a plausible explanation for what just happened. "Maybe what I thought was an octopus arm was something off the deck. That would be easier to believe, wouldn't it?"

He got up and looked around on the deck but saw nothing. "No, it wouldn't. If she got knocked off, then why didn't you rescue her? I tried!" He tried to defend himself as if he were in a court of law being cross-examined by a prosecutor while being tried for the possible murder of Candace Cotton. He remembered the Lacy Peterson case, except that SOB was guilty. He sat in the recliner Candy had been sitting in earlier. Her fragrance still lingered, and he inhaled deeply, "Oh, Candy!" he cried.

CHAPTER 6

By morning, the boat had been drifting all night. He had not started the engine since he and Candy turned it off yesterday. He wasn't ready to go yet and was still hoping that maybe something would surface. He wanted Candy to come back, that's what he really wanted, maybe she is still alive just out of view. No, he wasn't leaving without Candy or the beast, one or the other. He started to think how maybe he could hook this thing and take back a piece of it. The thought of ever seeing it again was terrifying, and he started wondering now what he was going to do if it did come back. He knew he needed proof that it really exists. He began to think; maybe he could get a piece of it, a tissue sample or something.

"How am I supposed to do that?" he asked himself when just thinking about it was scary enough, "Now, if I had a gun or cannon, maybe." He sat down, put his face in his hands, and pushed back his sun-bleached hair. He needed a weapon and a plan. It occurred to him that one way to prevent any persecution of him was to prove the existence of this giant monster. "Funny nobody ever saw you!" he yelled toward the giant octopus. "Why is that? How can something as big as you stay hidden?" he asked. "Are you scared! What are *you* scared of!" he yelled louder at the water. "Where did *you* come from? You are an *abomination* to all other animals, and you don't belong here!"

He started trying to remember if he had ever heard of any such creature as this in these waters. He was sure he hadn't. It began to get hot, and he hadn't seen another boat since they got here yesterday. Brad's water was starting to run low, so he started drinking the beer, and by evening, he was crying again. He picked up his guitar, strummed the strings, and checked the tuning. Turning a couple of keys, he strummed a few notes. He was thinking of their song, "Come to Me," by Goo Goo Dolls. He started with a C and then F, G, it was coming to him.

He started to sing as tears filled his eyes, "Come to me, my sweetest friend, can you feel my heart again. Take me back where we belong. This can be our favorite song," and finished with, "And when we're old and near the end, we'll go home and start again."

He liked singing to her. She thought he could have been frontman in a band, she had told him that before. He was feeling extremely romantic after they made love one night, got up, and typed a chorus to a song he was working on into his laptop. He thought of it as a country waltz. He was working on the chords still, but he remembered the words. He sang them to himself quietly: "Thank you for making the life that I'm living, worthwhile with your giving, yourself to me. And thank you for showing the love that I'm knowing, your heart light is glowing with your love for me."

He wanted it to be about her anyway. He continued to strum for a little while. He had another favorite that he thought described her quite well, but he didn't play it for her. It would probably make her mad if he did, although she would have had to agree with him that it did describe her. He played it when she wasn't around, Tom Petty's "Wildflowers": "You belong among the wildflowers, you belong on a boat out at sea." He stopped there. She was a wildflower, but he couldn't sing this song anymore. He looked out across the darkening sky, and it suddenly made sense what he had to do.

"I can't go home again. I'm not going home again, not unless I catch you. I'm going to catch you!" He looked out over the bow where he last saw Candy and yelled into the water, "I'm going to catch you, you *hear*! You giant, *wuss*! You're a puss who acts like a wuss! That's why nobody ever saw you! YOU'RE A WUSS."

The beer was affecting him now. He got another and kept at it. "YOU TRIED TO STAY HIDDEN, DIDN'T YOU? HAHA! BUT YOUR LITTLE SECRET IS OUT. YOU'VE BEEN FOUND OUT ABOUT, AND DO YOU KNOW WHAT THAT MEANS?! IT MEANS YOU, MY NOT-SO FRIENDLY NEIGHBORHOOD KRAAAAKEN, WILL HAVE TO DIE!"

He turned from the boat edge and started looking around. "I'm going to catch you, you motherf'er WUSS! Wuss! The wuss from hell! I'm going to bring you in. I'm coming after YOUUUU, WUSSSS!" he yelled from the boat, "Or I'm going to die trying," he said softer. "You can't make octopus shit out of my sweetheart, you bastard!" He tossed the empty bottle over the side. "There! I hope that hits you on whatever you call your head!" he called into the now dark waters. "WAKE UP DOWN THERE! DO YOU HEAR ME! DO YOU!" he yelled into the waters. He grabbed another beer and started checking to see what he had around he could use to catch a giant octopus. He knew he must be ready if he comes back up tonight. "I'm not afraid of you, you spineless piece of shit throwback to damn dinosaur days. WUSS! YOU HEAR ME! YOU ARE NOTHING!" he yelled at the waves slapping the boat, "YOU DIE TONIGHT! OH YES! YOU ARE GONNA DIE!" and threw another bottle over the side. "There! A depth charge! BOOM!" he yelled as it made its way to the bottom. "Wuss the puss is gonna be dead tonight!" he said under his breath. He sat down to think about what else he could do.

He remembered the Ernest Hemingway book *Old Man and the Sea* and the tribulations he endured. He remembered watching the movie with Spencer Tracy as his hands were cut by the fishing line and bled as he tried to bring the enormous sailfish in. He would not have those same issues except sharks, that was a problem for Spencer Tracy, if he remembered correctly.

He hated the thought of having to deal with sharks too. He was not trying to bring this monster in for food but just for proof of its existence. Still, he knew it was not going to be easy.

CHAPTER 7

At the marina, John was checking around the dock to see if Brad and Candy had made it back, but no one had seen them. He went back to his office and tried the cell phone number Brad had left, but it went to voicemail. Next, he picked up his own phone and called the Coast Guard shack not far from there.

"This is John, hey! I haven't heard nothing from that couple who went out on an overnight trip. They were supposed to be back before dark."

"Okay," was the response.

A few minutes later, two Coast Guard pickup trucks pulled into the marina. Reports were filled out, including all the info they had left with John, including his next of kin, on the forms that were required to be kept there, and they asked about any witnesses who saw them last or who might know where they were headed. He recounted to the officers his last conversation with Brad about the phones.

"I tried to call him, so either their phones died, or

they are at least twenty miles out," he went on, "They could have broken down, but that's a new boat . . . never had any trouble with it."

The officers phoned in the boat's name, *The Cotton Candy*, her description, registration number, and a few other details to aid in the search; then they left. A thirty-three-foot Coast Guard patrol boat was called and dispatched to the area to where the Boston Whaler was supposed to be headed with search-and-rescue orders. Additional resources were called, including a rescue helicopter.

CHAPTER 8

"Bait?! What do I have that giant octopuses like to eat?" He looked, but he could find nothing. "I'M SORRY, WUSS, BUT YOU ATE MY LAST FIANCÉ LAST NIGHT!" he yelled toward the ocean.

He wasn't able to find anything even though he didn't know what he was even looking for. They didn't bring that much anyway, and now he had nothing, and that thing could be as big as a whale. Then it hit him. "A harpoon!" he said out loud. "I've got two wooden paddles and rope on board. I'm going for it," he said, then procured the two paddles from their rack and found the large butcher's knife he had brought to trim the steaks.

He began to hack at the edge of the flat end of the paddle. He was starting to make a point. He cut and chopped at the end until he had cut a very nice point, and with the tip made of hardwood, it became lethal. He backed up a few inches and began cutting a second cut to create a splinter effect that would be difficult to pull out once it got under the skin of the creature. He was determined and focused now that he had a plan. He had plenty of strong nylon rope on board, but he couldn't find a way to tie the rope onto the paddle, so he began drilling a hole with the tip of his knife into the paddle handle end. It took much longer and was darker when he got the first harpoon ready.

A cool chill engulfed him, and he shook with anxiety. He picked up the second paddle and began hacking at the end when he noticed the clouds had gotten heavy and darkness surrounded him. He was starting to get tired, and his bravery began to diminish as he was sitting in the lounge chair with his eyes wide open and his hearing focused toward the waters. Every splash caused him anxiety as he felt exhausted but couldn't relax. He couldn't stop looking into the darkness where he imagined every white top of a wave was the creature breaching the surface undetected. His tired eyes wearily darted from white tip to white tip as every motion caught his eyes.

It was cooler tonight, he noticed, and he wondered if the sea monster was even coming back up tonight. Maybe not, it may be miles from here. "Oh, Great Pumpkin, no one is going to believe you exist if they don't see you." His thoughts of Linus, the *Peanuts* character, led him back to thoughts of Wuss, which made him think of Candy. Maybe Wuss wasn't the only wuss around here, and maybe he was scared of more than just Wuss; he began to wonder now as he felt the stabbing pain of loss and heartache building in his chest again. How could he ever have thought he could leave her? He now knew for sure that he would have come running back. He couldn't have withstood the self-inflicted pain that his leaving would cause himself. If he didn't want to live without her, how could he ever have walked away, even if he became bold enough to threaten to leave her? None of it made any sense. What do you do when you know it's over but you still love her?

The beer and the hot sun left him with a headache. He was feeling a little dehydrated, so he drank a lemonade drink as he sat there thinking about Candy and how he was going to tell her mother and Chris what happened. He thought again that it probably didn't matter anyway, he probably wasn't going to survive if it does come back. He remembered it better now seeing suction cups, a lot of them, and around each suction cup, he'd swear he saw teeth, and each suction cup was as large as a coffee cup. It all happened so fast. They were big enough to easily see now that he's had time to recover a little from the shock and recall the beast in more detail as he could remember. He needed to know what he was going up against. He lay there thinking about it and began to fall asleep but was startled awake by a loud noise.

"Brad!" Certain he heard Candy call his name, he opened his eyes. It was dark, and the wind was picking up. He looked at the stars and remembered just last night, he and Candy made love right here. Her scent still seemed to linger here, or he supposed he might just be imagining it. Tears were beginning to fill his swollen red eyes again when he heard the first splash near the boat and sat up quickly, wide awake now.

He picked up the harpoon with the rope attached to it with the other one nearby. The fish jumping increased, and suddenly noise from the water rushing all around him became louder. Out about twenty feet on the starboard side, he saw it break the surface. A tentacle that could probably reach the boat from right where it was had breached the surface and was whipping over its body. A tremendous splash sent a wake that shook his boat, but Brad held tight with both feet planted.

"Oh my god! What was I thinking?!" he yelled and began to pray, "Dear Lord, please forgive me for my sins. Please, Lord, by the blood of my Lord Jesus Christ, please forgive me." The next wave surge brought the creature closer. "OH MY! OH MY!" he remembered he kept saying over and over.

"Gotta getta grip, Brad!" he said to himself, "You got no choice! You gotta do this or you're going to die, not him! No way is that monster getting me or anyone else."

He finally found his resolve and took a deep breath. He noticed his arms stopped shaking, and he had a vice grip on the harpoon handle. He felt his blood surging through his body. He was tense all over, every muscle in his arms, abdomen, and legs was rock hard. He was as ready to attack as any warrior who finds the courage when he thought he had none left to do what he had to do. He could feel fear rising up his neck; tears were making it difficult to see. He stood on the starboard side where he saw him last and held on to the side of the windshield with one hand while he leveled the weight of the homemade harpoon in his other.

The side of the boat exactly where he was standing began to rise out of the water. Brad crouched to help stabilize his balance and watched it up close; it was gigantic. He froze for a moment, but then slowly he brought up the harpoon. He didn't have a good shot; it was too low against the boat. He couldn't waste his one chance and have it just glance off. He knew getting a chance like this anyway was pure luck and doubted he would get another, so he couldn't just throw it and miss; he had to get a lethal shot.

The boat dropped back onto the surface of the water with enough force to throw Brad off his feet, but he held tightly to the harpoon as the water became rougher around them. Suddenly a powerful burst of water flew past his head with a loud "Choo!" sound like what a dolphin spouting spray might sound like. This was a real snoot full of water spray from the siphon of the squid. If it would have hit him squarely, it would have knocked him right off the boat. He didn't know it could do that, but it went down with the boat underwater again and came back up with the wave and another powerful blast of water came in Brad's direction like a fireman's water cannon but twice as powerful. Brad blocked some of it using the arm with the raised harpoon as he held onto the windshield frame with his other hand. He brought his harpoon down when he saw the monster had shifted his position. He needed to be patient to try and get a better shot. The creature was closer to the boat now.

Brad leaned over the side, and what he saw paralyzed him. The enormous creature was coming to the surface. Brad figured he was coming up to get a good grip on him with his little shark teeth. Then the unbelievable happened; the monstrous head started to rise out of the water. Brad couldn't move, although his legs were tense, he still couldn't move them. He knew he was about to slide off the boat at any second, so he held on with one hand to something attached to the boat at all times. He began to see part of the eye as it would dip down with the motion of the boat on the waves and come back up again. Brad raised his harpoon as the side of the boat sank down. The head, with an eye the size of a dinner plate, surfaced; it reached a tentacle high and swept the bow. It did exactly what he had seen it do when Candy was standing there.

"It remembered," Brad said and calmed down a little. He was pretty certain he must remember where his last meal came from. He turned around as the weight of the creature pulled down on the side of the boat even more. It looked like it was trying to climb in.

That's when he saw the entire thing looking back. "Hey, WUSS! You have to ask permission to come aboard!" he yelled at the huge eye. "Did you come here to invite me to dinner?" Brad yelled again but saw no reaction, no response, no empathy, nor remorse in the dinner plate–sized eye of the creature that looked like it didn't have an eyelid or brow. "What's the matter, you can't hear me? Did that big ole eye take up all your ear space? Do you have a brain in there or just more eye?" He moved around to get position, taunting it, knowing it had to see him with that enormous eye, "Huh?" It had no way to show expression and looked to Brad as if it was as innocent as he was. It was just looking in the same place he found dinner last night.

Brad thought it didn't look healthy either, but it was so scary anyway it didn't matter. He didn't know the giant had been starving up until last night. Now its strength was returning, and he was ready for another meal. Hunger changed his behavior and brought him to the surface looking for more food and hunger, which is what caused him to attack Candy. Brad knew what he had to do, and for a moment, he felt regret in the thought of it, but he was going to kill him if he could. He didn't want to. He knew he'd rather be watching him at SeaWorld, and he said out loud, "You're a man-eater now, Wuss!"

He broke his stare at the creature and glanced down at the deck to find footing. He was sitting down, but he had the harpoon at the ready when he saw the eye come above the railing for the first time and finally had the clean shot he was hoping for. He jerked himself up, got his feet set, turned loose of the railing, and with both hands, reared back and jabbed the makeshift harpoon with all his strength into its eye. It went in over a foot deep, but the monster lunged and snapped at him; he could see inside its grotesque beak.

He ducked and fended off the arms of the creature,

reached down, and picked up the last of his hand-carved weapons to attack the monster with and shoved it into that opened beak and quickly jumped back out of the way of the pink gross searching mass. He began to think about how ironic that in 2017, he still had to use a hand-cut harpoon to kill a sea monster. He thought about his *30 06* lying under his bed at home, "or the gasoline in the spare tanks!" He just thought of that but quickly dismissed it. He was sure he'd catch the boat and himself on fire. The rope had enough slack to reach the monster from the first harpoon strike. The shaft sank into the monster's eye up past the frayed portion. He felt like it should hold, but he didn't know how he was going to finish killing it, if that big poke in the eye didn't do it, before it destroys the boat. He heard cracking of railings and the windshield area was mostly gone. It seized up and gripped the boat, pulling down hard on the side.

That's when his first big mistake occurred. He wasn't expecting such a sudden violent jerk on the big boat, and it catapulted him to the railing and he flipped right over it. When he hit the water, terror set in, and he started thrashing to get to the surface. A tentacle found his leg and bit him, another bite and another as it pulled him underwater. He saw a piece of the rope and grabbed and held on as he began shaking violently in the cool waters. The squid turned him loose for a second, and Brad came back to the surface and grasped the side of the boat. In his mind, he knew the creature was wounded, and it looked like the hook was holding for now. Hopefully it was enough.

"Oh no, you don't! You aren't going anywhere." He quickly grabbed the end of the rope, dove under the boat, and began wrapping the rope around the propeller shaft. Just as he was making a couple of final wraps, it pulled tight. The back of the boat whirled violently around, and a sharp propeller edge caught Brad in his temple. He felt his head as a big knot was forming and he was bleeding and dazed. He knew he had to get back in the boat and again grabbed the back of it when he noticed it was floating freely with no tension on the line. He grabbed a railing, got a leg up, and started to get to his feet. Then he felt a tentacle wrap quickly like a whip around his waist. It pulled hard, but he hung on to the boat and started flailing at the huge arm around him. He looked for anything he could find to use as a weapon and saw the knife he had used to carve the harpoon out with. He had to take two steps to reach it, which meant he would have to turn loose of the only thing keeping him in the boat. He felt he had to, it already had him, and he could feel its jagged teeth on those suction cups cutting into his flesh and couldn't take it any longer. He pulled and pulled the immense arm along and felt the muscle around him pulling back hard. His breathing was harder, and his diaphragm was being crushed. He turned loose of the boat rail, took one final lunge, and reached the knife, but it came with a cost. He wasn't holding on to anything, and the arm jerked him back easily.

He began to stab it, but he only felt it tighten more around his torso, and it continued to tighten until he felt something pop. The arm picked him up and carried him right over the side. He could see as he was being carried away that the harpoon was still in its bloody messed-up eye, and he was still hooked. He hit the water and felt another tentacle wrap around him. He was pulled underwater and opened his eyes trying to see in the blurry waters. He frantically started reaching for anything and found the rope with slack and pulled his way hand over hand back to the surface. He tried to relax for a moment, but the boat suddenly jerked again. It was pulling the boat as it was trying to get away. That's when he made a break for the boat ladder on the other side and quickly discovered he could barely swim, something inside of him might be broken. He could hardly breath as well and pain stabbed his chest as he reached up to grab a rail. The boat started floating freely again.

Brad looked back as he made it to the ladder and saw a tentacle moving swiftly and sweeping the back of the boat. He ducked back behind the ladder but was still knocked back in by a glancing blow of the giant arm. He knew it was dangerous to be in the water with this thing. He grabbed for the boat, but this time the slippery creature was in his way. He struggled and continued to stab the slimy appendage. He saw the harpoon handle swing his way; he grabbed hold and twisted it into Wuss's eye deeper. He felt it penetrate the firm tissue as it thrashed its tentacles and struck a solid blow to Brad's head. He couldn't stop himself from falling, his body slumped, and he was stunned as he fell back and gulped the salty water. He stabbed hard one last time into the tentacle wrapped around him and left the knife there.

The monster was hurt badly, and he was able to push the tentacle away. His sinuses were burning terribly, his head had been hit hard, and his eyesight was blurred. Brad wanted to get on the boat, but his strength was gone, so he clung to the rope up near the boat motor and wrapped it around his arm. That's when he started shaking again and realized how cold he was.

CHAPTER 9

At the Coast Guard station, an investigator was sent to ask around about the two. She wanted to interview those who last saw the couple together to determine their state of mind. She stopped at the diner where the two had lunch last and was told by staff members that a few of the customers were concerned that these two were having difficulties and the man was none too happy with the woman's drinking and party habits. "Could it be something more than someone running out of gas or getting lost, maybe?" the waitress implied.

The officer finished the interviews and returned to her office to radio the ship en route to search a predetermined grid based on latitudes and longitudes in the area where the vessel may be. She recounted in her talk to witnesses at the diner that it's possible some domestic altercation may have transpired, but she didn't elaborate. "There is nothing criminal in either of their backgrounds. Just be aware," was her call. At 4:00 a.m., the helicopter pilot spotted the vessel just south of their projected heading. He radioed the patrol boat, which sped there posthaste. On arriving, the captain of the patrol boat called to the apparently abandoned fishing boat. The spotlight illuminated the pieces of the vessel broken and hanging in the water. The captain had been patrolling these waters for four years now and had never seen a boat torn apart twenty miles from shore. The hairs on his neck stood up as he looked into the darkness over the vast ocean waters. Small waves slapping the boats made hearing difficult.

"Ahoy!" the captain called out, "Anyone on board!" The quiet was disheartening as he continued to sweep the ocean with the experienced gaze of someone whose life may depend on spotting danger in the darkness. He gave the order to board the vessel for any ideas of what had happened here. The busted-up vessel had smears of something sticky and black, and the odor was strong of fish to the point of pungent although there was no evidence of fish having been on board. "Anything?" he asked his boarding party. "No, sir, Captain."

Wanting to see for himself, he boarded the boat. The captain could see Petty Officer Smitty leaning over the side of the motor into the water. He had spotted a rope wrapped around the motor above the propeller. Just as he gave a pull on the rope, he saw a head drift around from the other side of the motor. "AAHH!" he gasped.

Everyone looked his way. "Over here, sir! I found somebody!"

"Let's get him out of there!" the captain ordered.

As they brought Brad's cold, rigid body, still unconscious, on board the bigger ship, the captain ordered the anchor of the smaller boat be brought up so the vessel could be towed in. On bringing the anchor line in, the boatswain caught a glimpse of what was on the end of it, dropped the line, and yelled. "Captain!" as his hands started trembling. "Captain! Sir! That's not an anchor line!"

CHAPTER 10

He woke in a hospital bed with his chest hurting. He could feel an elastic support wrapped around his torso and an IV needle in his arm with a bag of fluids hanging on a wheeled rack. He tried to move, but intense pain shocked him still. He took another breath, easier this time, and believed he felt okay other than his ribs and he had to pee. He eased back the covers and saw he was cleaned up and wearing a hospital gown. He held tightly to the bed railing and slid his feet to the floor. He was able to stand, so he gingerly made it to the bathroom pushing the IV pole ahead of him, pulling the electric cord on the IV pump from the wall socket.

On his way back, he saw two bags on the floor. One had Candy's purse in it, and inside that was her phone. He picked it up and saw the screen was dark, but he pushed the "ON" button anyway, lights flashed for a moment but then went off again. The battery was dead, just like on his phone, but he found the phone charger in the other bag. He felt another bite of pain course through his midsection as he bent down and pushed the phone plug into the wall outlet. He lay back down looking at nothing on the ceiling, wondering about "WUSS." Where is it now? The bloodied enormous eye was there in his mind's eye. It wouldn't go away like the eye of a monstrous shark close to your face; you can't unsee it in your mind. It is even there now in the peripheral field of his mind's eye, watching him.

He was trying to remember what happened. Last thing he remembered was not a rescue vessel, so he must have been unconscious when he was found. Who found him? He remembered hours had passed and he couldn't get back into the boat and clung to the rope wrapped around the propeller with his head barely above water. The squid was there too, but it had finally died from the harpoon's damage, and it was still hanging from the rope he was clinging to.

Brad remembered the last time he saw it. Its eye had almost been pulled out of the socket and that was the last thing he remembered clearly, but now he was so tired that he drifted back off. He awoke again when he heard a knock on the door. It was his daughter, Dee, smiling at him as she walked over to the bed.

"Dad? Are you okay?" She leaned over and gave him a big hug. It hurt but he didn't say anything. "I'm fine, sweetheart. How are you?"

"I'm good," she answered and sat next to him. "The hospital called me and told me you were here. I saw that thing you caught. It was on the news. You can pull it up on your computer, there's a big picture."

"Okay, I will later," he said. "It knocked Candy off the boat," he tried to say but couldn't quite finish and reached for Dee. He pulled her tightly to him and started sobbing loudly, holding tightly to his daughter. "I couldn't see her anywhere, Dee! I would have gone in after her, but I didn't see her anywhere!"

"It's okay, Dad," and Dee hugged him back until he composed himself.

They were just sitting there when the nurse came in, and seeing he was awake, she asked, "How are you feeling this morning, Mr. Reno?"

"Very beautiful," he answered, wiping his eyes, trying to remember the line from the *Rocky* movie when asked how *he* felt after being pummeled by Apollo Creed. His face was swollen, and his skin was still pale and wrinkled from being in the water all night.

"Any pain?" the nurse asked.

"Only when I breathe," he answered.

"Here, take this."

He dutifully accepted the pill and cup of water to wash it down with. "Who's this?" she asked, looking at Dee.

"That's my daughter, Dee."

"Hi Dee, it's nice to meet you. I'm Debbie!"

"It's nice to meet you, Debbie." Dee answered.

Dee visited for a while longer and said she had to get home to take her dogs out. She hugged her dad, said goodbye, and left. Brad dozed and woke an hour later a little clearer headed, got up to go to the bathroom again, and saw Candy's phone still plugged into the wall. He picked it up and saw it was charged now. His thoughts went back to this person he had never met but hated, Omar, the man who wanted Candy, and she must have wanted him. He felt another lump in his throat as tears welled up in his eyes. He just shook his head in disbelief as he turned the phone on and watched it light up, then punched in her code, and it opened up to her texts. He found Omar's name and opened the messenger to text him.

He started out, "Do you know Candy Cotton?"

The text came back, "Yes."

Next, he texted, "Did she tell you she was engaged?"

A pause, then, "No."

He sat there trying to figure out why she would behave so differently when she was around him. He kind of understood how she could lose her mind in a drunken stupor and go off with some guy in the back of his car, but she was stone-cold sober and gave this guy her phone number. He shook his head trying to understand who Candy was. His phone chimed in another text; it was from Omar. "I hope you haven't spent a lot of money on her," it said. He didn't answer, but in his mind, at least $50,000 over two years, but he wasn't going to tell this guy.

The tone chimed again, and the text said, "I wouldn't spend any more money on her."

"I won't be," he said to himself and ended the call. The phone went back to menu, and he saw she had other messages. "Who is Brian?" and he opened up the text. "Oh my god! She was seeing this guy too!" He read,

"Great time with you in Atlanta last week." He looked at the date when he texted this message. "Well, damn," he couldn't help but say out loud. "When I thought she was visiting her mother, she took a little detour!" He continued reading, "I made reservations at the Conrad Hilton in Atlanta on the 4th. It'll be wonderful," he finished. "Lots of fun! Can't wait!" she had texted back.

Brad turned the phone off as he realized his grief-stricken, heart-broken life had all been a big lie. He was ripped apart, and grief hit him hard, and he felt like something inside him had died. He sat down on the edge of the bed when another light rap on the door came. It was an officer in uniform.

"Can I help you?" Brad asked.

"Yes, sir, I'm Officer Durden, and I came by to ask you a few questions and fill out some paperwork if you're up to it. I was here earlier, but you were still asleep."

"Okay," Brad answered. "Can you tell me how I got here?" Brad asked.

"Yes! Sure, Mr. Reno! A Coast Guard helicopter brought you in about six this morning. I saw that thing you killed, Mr. Reno. I have never in my life seen such an animal as that," he said, still astounded. "And you caught him just twenty miles offshore here?" he asked more out of amazement and curiosity than a police officer filling out forms.

"Yes, about that," Brad said, and they went on to talk for an hour.

The officer mentioned that his doctor told him Brad

had at least six broken ribs. Then the officer asked him what had happened in his own words. It sounded like a real monster movie even coming out of his own mouth. He told him how Candy had called him to show him how the fish were jumping all around the boat, and then he described how Wuss's tentacle swept across the bow of the boat, without warning, taking Candy with it.

"Wuss? You called it Wuss?" the policeman stopped writing and showed a nervous smile, as he scrawled the name "Wuss" in the corner of his notes. "How did you come to call him that?" Brad replied, "Yes, well, at first I thought it was an octopus and I kept calling it to come back." "You wanted it to come back?" the policeman asked.

"Yes, I decided I wasn't going to leave until I killed it or it killed me . . . but it wouldn't come back to fight me, so I called it Wuss the Puss."

Officer Durden liked this guy. He had seen Wuss, and it didn't look like any wuss to him; it had measured over thirty-two feet in length, and the body was at least ten feet in circumference. It had eight arms and two tentacles with razor-sharp teeth embedded in the suction cups, up and down all of them, and the beak of this thing was over twenty-two inches from front to back. He had heard the scientists examining it trying to put into perspective the damage something like that can do. One compared it to the chipper that tree surgeons use to turn limbs into wood chips, and no bones can withstand it and said even much-smaller squids have been known to amputate limbs. The officer had to give the guy credit; he took it out. Brad began to tell how he searched and searched for Candy. He told Officer Durden how he swore he wouldn't leave her. He started crying again. That's when the officer stood up.

"That's enough for now, Mr. Reno," he said. He had to do a few things and he may be back to talk some more.

"That's fine," Brad said.

Officer Durden knew how close he had come to dying out there. He just assumed Brad was still in shock.

From the way the Coast Guard medic described his condition when they found him, he would have died soon from hypothermia even without the other injuries. The officer didn't suspect foul play, so he finished his report with pictures of the boat and the creature included. He wrote how the only witness, Mr. Reno, had seen Ms. Candace Cotton swept off the boat by the giant squid and, after being unable to locate her, decided to stay and fight the monster he had named "Wuss" should it come back, which he had no way of knowing. He decided to use this name himself to indicate this creature when he referred to it because he liked the spirit in which it was given. Mr. Reno was able to kill "Wuss," and the carcass of the animal was brought to St. Peterburg's morgue for dissection. As the usually cool-headed officer was about to leave, he stood up and walked over to the bed.

"Mr. Reno?"

"Yes, sir," Brad answered.

"Mr. Reno. That was incredible . . . what you did."

He reached out to shake Brad's hand as he repeated the name Brad had given him. "A thirty-two-foot sea monster . . . and you named him"—he couldn't contain his smile—"Wuss." Brad didn't smile. "Do you know what the Mexicans around here call it?" Brad shook his head gently. "Diablo Rojo. Know what that means?" He shook his head again. "Red Devil, Mr. Reno. Red Devil, and you called him Wuss. It was a great pleasure to meet you, sir. I believe there is a reporter who would like to talk to you. Just tell her what you told me. If you think of something else you want to add, please call me first."

"Okay, Officer Durden."

The door opened, and for a second, Brad thought it was Candy coming in. A beautiful blonde with about the same build as Candy came walking in. Her eyes were arctic blue and stunning, and he started shaking.

"I'm Crystal Brook, from WPBG News out of St. Petersburg, Mr. Reno."

As she walked toward the bed, she switched the microphone she was holding from her right to her left hand as if she wanted to shake his hand but then decided not to offer her hand and she was not smiling. A man with a camera on his shoulder came into the room behind her.

"This is Levi, he's my cameraman. May we film you while we talk?"

"Well, I guess so . . .," Brad said. He really didn't feel like it right now, but here they were. "Tell us how all this happened?" she started.

"What?" Brad asked, unsure of what she was asking.

"What happened to Candace? What happened to Candace Cotton, Mr. Reno?"

"What?" Brad looked at her not knowing where to start. He wanted to know the answer to that question himself. He wanted to say, "I wish I knew," but that's not what this reporter wanted to hear about.

"Mr. Reno? Have you heard yet that they dissected the giant squid?"

Brad froze, and his eyes locked on hers as he listened intently.

"We just left there a few minutes ago, Mr. Reno." She paused to get his full attention. "They found human remains in the stomach. How do you feel about that?" She pointed the handheld mic in his direction.

He sat up a little as a swell of pressure built up quickly behind his eyes. He was trying to hold it in, to hold his breath, and that made his ribs hurt. His eyes began to turn red and fill with tears as he dropped his head into his hand and wept. He was hoping that was not the case. That means she most likely had been alive as this frightening beast was devouring her, and he suddenly felt sick. Crystal wanted to get off this topic now.

"They have sent for dental records and have kept samples for DNA testing to be done immediately. They tell us four to six weeks on that."

He took a napkin off his tray table, wiped his eyes, and then blew his nose. He held on to the napkin, and without apologizing for his tears, he looked at her.

"You look enough like her, I thought you were her when you walked in, caught me off guard." Crystal blushed. "Do you want to ask me some questions?"

Suddenly the usually assertive and sometimes brazen questioner paused. She watched him composing himself. He looked up at her and said, "Okay, go ahead."

Her straightforward demeanor had changed some. Before she spoke again, she remembered the animal lying in the morgue that had partially devoured a human being, a woman—a woman who looked like her. She remembered seeing the dismembered body pouring out of the enormous stomach. She saw it, it made her puke, and it made her mad, but she looked anyway. She wasn't the only one to puke. She saw how it looked as remains poured out of the creature and the smell was gut wrenching, with fish parts and hard shells mixed in. It looked like she was sliced up with sharp knives, not chewed up and swallowed by some animal, and she was certain this was not the whole story. She wanted answers, so she began her questions focusing on the location where the creature was found. She wanted to know why they were there and what they were doing. He told her about the condo and boat slip there and of the overnight excursion they had planned. He smiled when he told her about the fish she fought with for ten minutes and then how they laughed about it for an hour after her line snapped. He told her about the steak dinner they had under the stars and the bottle of wine. He told her it had been perfect up until later.

Crystal felt like she had reason for her skepticism.

Before she came to the hospital, she had asked around and had heard about the strained conversation Brad and Candy had at the restaurant before they left. She told Brad she had talked to them, and a few witnesses, including the waitress who served them, had suspected something bad might have happened.

"Yes," he countered her assertion, "I found a monster and had him knock Candy off the boat. I'm sorry, would you please rephrase the question because something bad *did* happen, 'Wuss' killed my fiancé!"

"Wuss?" she cut in.

"Yes," he said, "that's what I called it."

He hadn't felt like talking, but now with Crystal going around looking for a motive for some nefarious deed here, he decided he would point a few things out to this conspiracy theorist news reporter. He wanted to tell her there is a great man-eating monster story here, which should be enough for any good reporter, but no, she wants a murder plot twist. She was here for the story within the story. He decided right then he would tell her a story, a monster story, or what he could remember about it.

"And why did you call it Wuss?" she asked and leaned forward to listen to his answer with a condescending look on her face.

He recanted the story he had told the officer about how he thought it was a giant octopus at first, then he stopped as he remembered something else, how frightened he was. Crystal saw the expression on his face change as he began remembering. Images of the monster's shiny tree trunk–size tentacles wrapped around him, squeezing every bit of air out of his body, flashed in his memory. He recalled the protruding bloody eye staring straight at him. This caused a chill to run through his body as he lay there remembering it so clearly. He remembered being so afraid that every nerve ending on his entire body was tingling, and he was shaking, even violently at times. His fight-or-flight dilemma was not a dilemma for him because he had nowhere to run. It became a fight-or-die dilemma. His main focus was on trying to keep his knees locked and not to fall off the boat as he was trying to harpoon this monster. He thought about Candy again and realized there was more to this question.

"I was frightened," he finally said. "I guess it helped give me courage, made me feel bigger than him . . . superior. I had to kill it if I could," he said, "I couldn't let my fear stop me." He looked up directly into the eyes of the reporter. "I had nowhere to go,"—his brow furrowed as he spoke with sincere passion—"and I couldn't leave Candy." He shook his head slightly as he felt sudden wave of sadness go all the way to his heart.

She could see in his eyes that there was no other choice and tears were running down both his cheeks now. "I had no escape plan, no plan B, so I called him Wuss . . . so I could . . . could gather the courage, I guess . . . to attack . . . *him.*" He didn't tell her that it was in his mind that without the carcass, it might be difficult for people to believe his story and thus be led to the wrong conclusion and that he had in fact murdered Candy. He didn't say that to this or any other reporter lest they run with the story and try to connect coincidences to figure out how he pulled it off. "Reporters," he said to himself and shook his head. That made his back start hurting again. "Do you mind if we finish this later? I'm not feeling so good right now?"

The reporter wasn't ready to leave. "I really was hoping to get a few more details," she explained. He looked at her and said, "Ms. Brook, after I fell in the water, I don't really remember much." He went on, "Wuss grabbed me around here"—he pointed around his waistline—"and squeezed me hard enough to break ribs which he did. He had me, but the harpoon stab I think eventually did him in. When I tried to get up, I knew something was broken. I had no strength to get in the boat, and I thought I would probably die too, right there. I wrapped my arm around some rope near the motor and . . ." The reporter picked it up from there. "So, Wuss had you cold and could have killed you at any time."

"I think he must have been close to death when I fell in. I don't think he tried to eat me." Crystal was good at reading people. She could separate fact from fiction in a person's story very quickly. That's how she got where she was. She looked at Mr. Reno like a scientist looking at lab results but not quite knowing what to make of him yet. She knew that you could tell by the look on a man's face how much hardship and disappointment he's had to endure. She's seen it plenty of times in the eyes of victims of hurricanes, murders, and traffic accidents.

When a man has lost the most important thing in his life, you may never see much more than a cordial smile on his face again. He only realizes his happiness and energy are connected, when he doesn't have either anymore. It made her sad to think that now for Mr. Reno, there will be a permanent sadness when he thinks of Candy that will linger in his heart for the rest of his life. Candy was gone, and there was no reason for him to even try to smile anymore. He didn't care; she saw it in his face that he loved her.

"Do you mind if we stop for now, Ms. Brook. I gave you the scoop of a lifetime. Man-eating sea monsters exist. That should be the story," he said a little more tersely than he meant. He couldn't look at her anymore, the resemblance to Candy was too striking. He turned away from her because he didn't want her to see he was tearing up again. She told him she would try to stop by tomorrow if he didn't mind. "I don't," he said, facing the wall. He could almost see Candy's face in hers.

CHAPTER 11

Dee came back by later and brought his computer. After several frustrating attempts and two trips to the nurse's station, he was able to pull up pictures of the monster. He was shocked that the headline included the name he had given it: "Wuss, a 32-Foot-Long Man-Eater Kraken, Killed 20 Miles off Florida's Gulf Coast." It had his name in there as the fisherman and the one who named him.

"Fisherman!" he said under his breath. It had Candace Cotton, from Mount Pleasant, South Carolina, listed as its only known victim and offered a few new facts he didn't know from the autopsy. First off, it was a male, and it had hundreds of the deadly razor-embedded suckers. Its eye, that he looked directly into, was nineteen inches across.

When she listed the known habitats of these creatures, she had a difficult time pinning any down. colossal squids are mostly found in the deepest waters of the world, waters exceeding two thousand feet deep.

It was not known how such an animal wound up twenty miles from the Florida coast. He didn't want to guess what else might be lurking down in the depths there. He certainly wasn't going to Antarctica to look for anything else; he turned off the laptop. On the day of his discharge, there was a knock at the door.

"Hello! Anybody home?" came the familiar voice of Crystal.

"Hi! Come in!" he said back as he picked up some clothes that were lying on the only chair in the room.

"Have a seat!" he offered.

"No thanks," she said, "I just stopped to see if you were really going home today?" "Yep!" he answered, "I've got a lot to catch up on."

"Oh, Okay, well, I was just stopping to, huh, suggest that I may like to do a follow-up story on you if you don't mind?"

"Well," Brad answered, "let's get a bite of lunch. I refused to eat breakfast this morning so I could go get a big juicy hamburger and French fries and a couple of ice-cold Coronas for lunch. You're invited to come along."

"I'd love to," she answered.

He caught her eye, and she smiled a little. "Okay," he said and held the door open for her. "Where are you going, Captain Ahab?" came a frantic call from his nurse down the hall. "I'm going home!" he said.

She pushed a wheelchair she had brought along with her up to him. "Hospital rules, you have to be wheeled out in a wheelchair, like it or not." She smiled and nodded at Crystal. "Crystal Brook, this is my nurse, Debbie. Debbie this is Crystal," he said. He sat down while Crystal said hi, barely able to contain her own smile, then she put her hand on his shoulder and walked beside him.

He pondered on his drive to the restaurant about how such a creature made it to the waters off St. Petersburg, Florida, but it was there. It seemed to Brad that there was always *one* of something around where it shouldn't be to ruin things. The world is a big place, and there's plenty of room for things to scatter.

While he and Crystal sat outside at a local popular restaurant having lunch; Brad watched a fly buzzing around their table. It reminded him of Candy. It seemed every time he and Candy ate outside on a veranda or porch, a fly would join them, just one.

"Now, how is that even possible?" he remembered asking Candy about it. She thought it was funny. He remembered her asking a waiter once when they went back to a restaurant where they had that annoying experience. "Oh, waiter? Can you tell me if our fly arrived ahead of us or will he be joining us later?" She could make him laugh. "There should be lots or none," he would say, "just like now with Wuss, there's either lots of these creatures or there should be none." He believed there were lots, just like flies.

PART TWO

BRAD RENO AND CRYSTAL BROOK CONFRONT MOASM

CHAPTER 12

Brad was preparing to lie down for the night on his fishing boat. He had finally decided to go back out on it and this was his first overnight trip since the attack by the colossal squid, he had named, Wuss. He was turning off lights and adjusting his radio to listen to some soft music when he heard a splash then another. It was pitch black and quiet just past the railing when suddenly the ocean waters exploded all around him. Something enormous and horrifying was coming up out of the black water and it slammed against his sturdy boat knocking him off his feet. He froze in fear as he forced himself to look up into the darkness. What he saw caused his mouth to drop open and his strength left him as the blood in his legs, retreated to his core. It took all his strength just to move them. He couldn't even lift his arms. He saw several thick, fleshy, pale-gray tapering arms of a monster rise above him in blurry contrast with the night sky. Moonlight glimmered off the lethal dripping suction cups that wanted to find and latch on to him and drag him to his horrific death. Like a flash of grotesque lightning, one was whipping downward toward his face, but Brad reflexively drew back like a batter's reflex causes him to move out of the way of the pitcher's fastball a split second before it takes his head off. An enormous giant squid tentacle landed hard on the deck just in front of him with a smacking wet slap. He winced at the strong smell of the sickening fishy-stench wafting over him from the slimy appendage. The size of the giant arm caused him to freeze in fear. There was nowhere to run and nowhere to hide. The large tentacle was creeping toward him on the deck, searching for whatever it could find to eat. Don't jump out of the boat, he kept saying to himself, although he would do anything to keep away from that tentacle. He remembered how the other one cut him up good. The undulating movement like a cobra kept rising up and slamming down on the wet deck in wave-like movements. The thick tip of the appendage was creeping closer toward him like it knew where he was and could sense his presence and his fear. The boat was listing as the slimy man-eater rammed its body up against the hull closer in an effort to extend its reach in its blind search. Fear was causing Brad to weaken and he was losing his grip. He struggled to hold the handrail as tight as he could. He was as far astern as he could get from this enormous searching, snaking, appendage that belonged to a beast he once thought was mythical but was here now, seeking him out, as if it knew he was here hiding all along.

His experienced mind couldn't help but quickly assess the length of the deadly weapon. He was sure it could reach him from where it was, it had to be over twenty feet long. He could see the various sizes of the jagged razor-sharp teeth that were embedded around hundreds of the circular-shaped suction cups cascading down the underside of the long arm. The deadly intent of the creature was unquestionable. He jumped just as the arm lifted up and lunged forward in an effort to find him. His heart was racing as he kicked at, it in an effort to discourage it, but he couldn't connect. It was coming for him and he had nowhere to go. He was trapped, "Aiiii!" he yelled, and lashed out again. He grabbed the makeshift harpoon but had no grip. He felt weak, he couldn't stand and his legs were like lead. Two of the massive arms were about to wrap around him. He sank backwards to escape and kicked and jabbed his feet forward at the frightening arms again and again. "Aaaaiii!" he yelled louder and lashed out in a defensive move but this time he was sure he was a goner until his own yell startled him awake.

Brad sat on the deck of his home overlooking the beautiful marshlands of the low country having coffee. He had mostly forgotten the details of his dream except he knew he had one because it had awakened him and he knew what it was about. He only had nightmares about one thing. It had only been a few months since the loss of the woman he loved, Candy Cotton, and the life and death battle with the with the 32-foot-long colossal squid that swept her off his small fishing boat during an overnight fishing trip in the Gulf of Mexico. The nightmares prove he was lucky and Candy was unlucky. If he had been standing where she was, it would have been him swept over the side by the massive fluid arm of this giant. He has had a few bad dreams like this where he had to fight the sea creature since coming home and in every attack, he knew he wouldn't have survived. He didn't feel lucky, he felt like someone who barely survived after getting the shit beat out of him and that didn't seem like luck to him. It should be him who was dead and he knew it, after all, it was his boat, he planned the trip, he picked the day and everything....and" he kept going, he was older, his kids were grown and his usefulness on the world in general was about over, but no, Candy was dead and it made him depressed to think about it. It was over now and everyone reassured him that it was a freak thing. He wasn't so sure but he was trying to get over it.

It came back to him how he had said a prayer before he began his battle with Wuss. He went to his bedroom and found his well-worn Spiritual Renewal Bible under a stack of papers. He didn't waste much time thinking about it, he decided he would just start reading and see how far he could get. Images of scenes depicted vividly in his mind's eye were long ago etched in his memories from childhood days in Sunday school and the gold stars his teacher used to give them for memorizing Bible verses. These memories of his childhood Sunday school classes began to flood his mind and refresh his memory with the people and lessons of the Bible. His questions to God were awkward and difficult to frame, at the same time, he felt like he had to try to understand to be able to accept and come to terms with Candy's death. He saw Candy swept off his boat right in front of him by a giant squid. How could anyone fit this image into their beliefs and feelings of the bigger picture the scripture promises. Was this her destiny? Well, it certainly was her fate. He imagined how that premonition would have looked in her yearbook. Candy Cotton, most likely to be, "eaten by a sea monster." Oh, and he had to imagine his picture beside her with the caption, "Brad Reno, most likely to stand there and do nothing while Candy Cotton gets eaten by a sea monster."

He had always been able to find some comfort in scripture. As a kid going to Sunday school, he had a great teacher. She would give out scriptures to memorize and gold stars on their certificates of completion. He had decided a long time ago that he thought it was a good idea to read the Bible. He rationalized it in the beginning by saying he didn't want to be standing before God someday and have to confess that he hadn't read it, so he read it from time to time to stay familiar with and to refocus his priorities. He skimmed quickly over familiar stories refreshing his memory with its cast of characters from Genesis to Proverbs but his mind had trouble staying focused. Then he read some of Isaiah, he had read it before but this time was different, he felt the need to read it again, with its familiar passages and exquisite detail, it would captivate his imagination and strengthen his faith but not this time. He felt like God had breached his, "Line in the sand." He had always heard that God didn't give people more than they could handle and he used to believe that until 9/11. He didn't think he could have handled having to decide to leap to his death or be burned up in either of those towers. That, Brad felt, would have been way more than he could have handled. When he mentioned that to his all-wise barber, she said, "Maybe that's why you weren't there," but he felt disconnected from God now. How could God have put a giant sea monster between him and Candy on a little boat? What was he supposed to do about that? How could he have saved her from that? "There was no way, no way," he said. The Bible's stories of disobedience and indiscretions abound, love and deceit, death, forgiveness and resurrection, it all comes down to each one of us individually having faith that the, "Good News," is all true, that Jesus walked out of that burial tomb on Easter Sunday and only God knows what he's doing now. He hoped that Candy was a true believer and he worried about that. He believed in God and Jesus the Son, but he was so frightened by this monster that it overwhelmed his senses. He couldn't imagine it but facing this creature had fundamentally changed him. He faced death but not without being traumatized, he was sure about that. He thought his faith was stronger too but he couldn't wrap his mind around what happened to Candy. He didn't think that was a very nice way for Candy to die. He was confused and a little angry below the surface. He felt like God owed him an apology or at least an explanation. "Sorry

Brad, someone had to be eaten by a sea monster." "Oh, okay," Brad could say and that would be that. It's God! In his nightmares the monster was always between him and Candy, he couldn't save her and knew God wasn't going to either. His focus on God became a reminder of Candy and how awful her death was and he wasn't sure she was in heaven. That was another question he had because her behavior was not that of your typical Christian believer. She liked booze and men and had enjoyed plenty of both in her 40 plus years. He wanted to believe she was in heaven but he really wasn't sure.

He's tried to get on with his life but there were still so many questions. There were questions that only God could answer mostly but there were more earthly questions as well, like, where did Wuss come from? How did a colossal squid get here? More importantly, are there more like that out there? He had no desire to go fishing anymore. He hadn't been back to Sanibel Island since he left.

By the time he got the chance to talk to Candy's mom, she had already learned what happened from-the police and coroner and realized the police and others saw him as a hero. He didn't feel like a hero. There was a rumor that one of the old fishermen at the docks had even given him the moniker, "Sea Monster Killer" when he couldn't remember Brad's name.

He took a walk down by the docks where shrimp boats come in and ran into an old friend of his dad's he had known since he was a kid. He owned a shrimp boat in Charleston for many years and knew every story and legend. Brad wanted answers to questions that Google couldn't answer but maybe this old guy could, like, how did he think a squid like Wuss, managed to get to the Florida coast?

The old fisherman was sitting on the deck of his trawler repairing a hole in a net when Brad approached his boat. Brad called his name and the old codger nearly turned his chair over trying to get up. "Hey Brad Reno! Well, where you been?" Brad thought it was funny. He made it sound like he had just been sitting there all day waiting for him to show up. "Hey Cap! How are you?" Brad yelled back. "Permission to come aboard?" he yelled. "Get your sandy bottom aboard you old landlubber! Ha Ha!" the old captain called. Brad boarded and handed the captain a bag with a bottle inside. "Arh, you know what I like don't cha my young mate?" Brad recalled a conversation they had before, "I remember you telling me a long time ago that the gift of a stiff drink with a friend can make a man stop work long enough to have a little talk and it does a lot to warm the soul and calm the sea. You laid it out clear just as you saw it." "Here," and he handed Brad a plastic cup, broke the seal on the bottle of Jack Daniels and poured them both about two fingers worth and recapped the bottle and set it on the table. He raised his cup to Brad and said, "A toast to you, my boy." He thought for a moment and began, "You may not be the best fishing boat captain around," he started his toast, smiled, walked over and put his arm around his long-time friend whom he loved like a son. "You may not be the most experienced fishing boat captain, either. Hell, you ain't even the handsomest fishing boat captain," he teased Brad, "that's who you are not, but do you know who you are? Huh?" he paused. "You are Brad Reno, Sea Monster Slayer, and the most famous of us all!" Brad started to move away. "No, just a minute young Brad Reno, do you know why I say that? Please don't take it as a cut or insult. No! I'm serious! You deserve the praise. I may never have told you this story. Did I ever tell you about alligator hunting?" "No, why?" Brad asked. "Because, I was asked to go on an alligator hunt one year. I was regretting it the moment the first gator got close to the boat." Brad could tell the old captain was serious. "I was scared to death all day. I wanted nothing to do with alligators as soon as the first one started ramming the boat but once you get out there, there is no turning around and going home. We slayed some big gators that day. Some as big as thirteen-foot from nose to tip of the tail. They don't die easy, nope, once you hook'em, you have to slay'em. That's why I called you that, Sea Monster Slayer, high praise my friend because that's what you did. You hooked 'im! You hooked him good. Any fisherman knows, when you hook the granddaddy, that's when the fight begins and you're going to have your hands full, but you, my fine young captain, brought the scallywag to heel and I know it was no little feat, young Brad Reno," he said again and raised his cup to his mouth and drank it all down.

"That brings up a question I had about that thing,"

Brad went on, "where do you think it came from? How did it get here?" The old fisherman poured them both another drink and put back on what he called his fisherman's, "thinking cap," and started thinking. "Well, I hadn't heard of or seen any in the waters around here. Pretty much had resigned to the idea that either they were just a myth or there just weren't any around here but if I had to say, I'd say it was carried with the current and could wind up most anywhere." He said the story surprised him but only because it took so long for someone to spot the next one. He explained that he had heard old sailor stories that had been handed down over the generations. "Not any lately that I know of. I don't remember when I last heard of one being spotted, so, I guess I'll just repeat the one story I can remember." He took another big sip of his drink before he started. "As I recall, this was the one I believed most, too. It goes something like this. In the days of old, heh," he laughed a little, "when sailors shoved off into the vast unknown, the unknown in those days was not only unknown, but it was believed that this unknown was inhabited by sea monsters." Brad could tell by the look on the old man's face that he was very serious. "Sea monster sightings were reported by some sailors but no one believed them much mainly because they had no proof they really existed in the first place, like dragons, for instance. So, all these stories were swept to the files of myths and legends...until the St. Mary. Sometime during the late 19th century, the cargo ship, St. Mary, started out on her regular journey right out of Charleston here to sail from port to port on her scheduled trade route throughout the Caribbean, heading first toward the Keys. Now, the story goes," the captain got quieter and lower as he began to remember the details, "as God's will would have it, in the late summer of that year, the St. Mary, was pushed off course and farther out to sea by an early season hurricane farther than this captain and crew had ever been. The crew was making repairs and trying to right her course after fighting strong sustained headwinds for several days. The captain admitted he had been unable to maintain a steady bearing. He wasn't familiar with how strong the Gulf Stream current was either and how it was assisting pulling them farther north. After weeks of slow progress, rationing of provisions and the fear of never seeing land again, guess what happened?" "What?" Brad asked with his gaze fixed on the old man. The fisherman got louder and started using his hands for accentuation and punctuation, "A... well...you have to call it a sea monster, Brad! That's what the only survivor said. A sea monster attacked and sank the St. Mary, and this survivor happened to also be the captain." The fisherman paused for emphasis. "He was thin and badly sunburned after being exposed to the elements for weeks and the exposure alone should probably have killed him but it didn't, so he described what he saw. The albeit dead captain said he saw a leviathan. Have you ever heard anyone use that word in a sentence before, Brad? As in, I saw a leviathan! It's a giant sea monster, Brad, like a Kraken! God said they were in the ocean. I never doubt the Bible," then he looked at Brad hard with his one good eye, "you believe everything in the Bible don't cha Brad?" he asked as the Jack Daniels was finding its mark and opening up the conversation exposing the old hard sailor's rough edges. Brad believed he would be a tough captain to work for. "I do," answered Brad. "I've got the scars to prove it." The old fisherman spewed a nice sip of Jack with that one. "You do, Captain Brad Reno! God said they were there and it took a good captain to bring back the carcass of one...and just like young Arthur, pulling the sword from the stone, you were the man to do it," he got quieter, "you're a good captain, Brad Reno, a mighty good captain," and raised his cup again followed by a big slurp of the whiskey he loved now more than fishing. Brad remembered thinking; this guy was probably great at telling his grand-kid's bedtime stories. The old fisherman continued, "An octopus-type monster with tentacles reached over the sides of his ship," the fisherman was waving his arms now to accentuate his point, "breaking masts and picking off crew members and eventually caused the St. Mary, to capsize. He swore it was of a size large enough to reach completely across the deck of the St. Mary, and sweep men and cargo overboard." He went on to say, "It had enormous octopus arms with hundreds of suction cups except these suction cups had razor-sharp, ivory-colored, ragged-looking teeth around the edges." He made a circle with his left-hand forefinger and thumb then placed his huge old jagged right-hand thumbnail behind it. "What does that remind you of?" "Well, it is hideous," Brad agreed. The old captain gestured and responded with a deep low, "Aye." Brad knew exactly what he was talking about, he was describing a giant squid. The old fisherman went on, "Then he looked out into the waters and he saw his men hanging on to overturned lifeboats and flotsam, being dragged down one at a time by enormous tentacles whipping and thrashing and slapping, pounding the ocean's surface." The fisherman stopped for emphasis; then went on, "That's when the captain realized something else and became even more terrified." "What?" Brad asked again. "Okay; here's what he said," the old man paused again and with his most serious look, flatly stated, "and this is why I believe him." He leaned over slightly so as not to be overheard. "There was more than one," the old fisherman said. "The captain, the only surviving witness to what happened, said there were hundreds of smaller ones. He said they were smaller but still big enough to carry a full-grown man down to Davey Jones' locker never to be seen again," he picked up his glass and finished the drink in the cup then reached for the bottle for one more shot. Brad believed him immediately and felt the need to sit down and the captain poured Brad another.

The fisherman went on, "Just one of these monsters, maybe fully grown maybe not, ripped the sturdy vessel to shreds. Men were screaming as they were being dragged down or so it stated in the official report given by the captain, being that he was the only eyewitness to the attack. The captain remained on board to go down with his ship but was later found by another cargo ship clinging to the only piece of flotsam he could find of the St. Mary. That piece of hull was what provided the means for him to survive but it was no surprise to him that he was the only survivor of this attack. His rescue and debriefing, so to speak, is where the legend began of the attack of the St. Mary. Many thought he was delusional. No one knew what happened to the cargo ship but that it had to be bad, evidence proved it had gone down and the captain was the only survivor. The captain, it was assumed, had lost his mind and had hallucinated the tale of the monster but many believed him to be a reliable man and not one prone to exaggeration. Family members of the crew that never returned were divided. Some believed and defended the captain while others were embittered and wanted the captain to hang. From that date on the legend was out there. The knowledge of even the possible existence of these creatures instilled fear in some including experienced seamen. It ended some careers while others just refused to accept they even exist and went about their business. Many thought sadly that the poor captain had lost his mind and gone "crazy" because all he could talk about for the rest of his devastated life was the, poor, St. St. Mary." Brad rightly assumed he would most likely have been lumped into the, "Crazy Captain," category too, or worse, if not for having the evidence of the monster carcass itself.

On his way home he couldn't get the story his old friend told him off his mind. "Poor, St. Mary," he said, as his imagination conjured up the raging battle of the men in the sea trying hopelessly to escape the deadly beasts. "Poor Candy," he said quietly. He was more convinced than ever that there are more of these creatures out there. What did the old man say? The last siting he can remember is over a hundred years old. That didn't sound right to him. He felt like there were a lot more out there and evidence had to exist and he was curious now.

At the funeral, Candy's mother was composed but it was apparent she was brokenhearted. No parent ever wants to bury their own child no matter the age. She was intensely grateful Brad was able to recover Candy's body. She began to cry and reached her arms around Brad. He began to cry as well and they did their very best to comfort each other. Brad had never met her brother but when he did, he didn't want a hug. He was not as forgiving and felt like Brad should accept more responsibility for the death of his sister. He had also heard the stories about the argument the two had at the restaurant before leaving for their overnight fishing trip. Brad could see an anger toward him just below the surface of his momentary stare. Brad kind of understood so he gave him his space. What happened was unbelievable even for him. They looked at each other but neither spoke.

Brad had gone back home after his tragic account in the beautiful waters off the west coast of Florida in the Gulf of Mexico. He stayed in his house for weeks going out only for groceries and to pay bills. The nightmares still would wake him some nights and other nights he cried himself to sleep. He couldn't stop thinking about what it must have been like for Candy. In his dreams he tried every way to rescue her but it was useless.

His whirlwind romance with Candy was tragic from the start. He loved her. He remembered telling her more than Romeo loved Juliet. He even remembered borrowing the pickup line from the song and using it on her, "You and me, babe, how about it?" from Dire Straits cover of Romeo and Juliet. She smiled, he melted, it was over for him, and he was a gone gosling.

He remembered their trip to NYC. They went to Rockefeller Center to a Rockettes Christmas show and to the Broadway Show, "Rock Star" in the Helen Hunt Theater. He remembered her smile and how excited she was to visit the small but eccentric restaurant, Serendipity, she had read about in a novel she enjoyed. He was recently reminded of that trip after watching, "Butch Cassidy and The Sundance Kid" with Paul Newman, again. He particularly remembered thinking of Candy while watching the scene where Butch, Sundance and Etta were in the city having what looked like a wonderful time with smiles and laughter, loud music with singing and dancing and great food. It was the last such time they all had together, sort of like his trip to NY with Candy. He started thinking about their visit to Battery Park to view the Statue of Liberty. His mind wandered back to her standing there smiling. The pleasant memory was interrupted when his mind's eye began to visualized giant tentacles coming out of the waters and feeling their way up and wrapping around the pale green statute and visitors were running and screaming as the statue crumbled and was being carried away by huge monstrous tentacles into the harbor to be lost forever leaving a wake of death and rubble on the empty base of the statue behind as Candy continued to smile for the camera.

He typed in, Wuss, in the Google search engine on his desktop computer. Amazingly, there was already an entire library of articles and ads in the drop-down list. He looked for one of the articles with a picture and found a bigger article with illustrations of the dissected body. An illustrator had drawn a picture of the creature with its body parts labeled. It was ugly no matter how you drew it. Stepping back a moment, he realized that it was also an incredible animal, the giant squid. He couldn't think of any animal on land that, without much visible differences, could range in size from an inch to what could only be described as "giant" growing as much as 65 feet in length. That was incredible, but even at half that size, Wuss was a killer unlike any other. He read on that as soon as a squid envelops its prey, it dives to the bottom of the ocean. He thought of Candy immediately, that's why he couldn't find her. She was already dead at the bottom of the Gulf of Mexico. He still hurt for her and every time this came to mind it reminded him of the unanswered questions he still had about Wuss. Where did it come from? How did it get here? Are there any more like him? Was he born here? He stopped, "Oh my God!" he said out loud. Somewhere he had read that these things can have hundreds of babies at one time. He realized nothing was certain but that was why he thought it was important. Where was he born? Find that place and he felt certain there were many more of these giants and that made him think that maybe he should tell someone.

Brad was sitting on his deck having his second cup of coffee. Two was his limit, the first was always the one he wanted, and the second satisfied his appetite and got him started in the mornings. He usually ate later. He was thinking about doing something today, but maybe he wouldn't. He was feeling a little low now. All the things he enjoyed doing when he was in his 20's and 30's are now no different than other fading memories. He thought about what he could be doing, there were a lot of activities around but he didn't feel like doing any of them. Going fishing or to the beach or the pool or to some restaurant just wasn't what he wanted to do. He wasn't even hungry although he still hadn't eaten anything. It was like he was done trying to please everyone, anyone, even himself by saying, "If I'm not hungry, I'm not getting up!" and for now that was his sentiment. He didn't feel the desire to be social or the need to entertain anyone. Why bother? If it's not one tragedy it's another. Life is a constant struggle. He had done really fun things in his past but now there isn't anything he wanted to do. His "bucket list," had become unimportant, irrelevant, so what if he never sees the top of the Alps or Himalayan Mountains from a plane. That's okay, now. Maybe it's another time or season as the old song goes and he began to sing quietly,

"To everything, turn, turn, turn, there is a season." And this was the time for a new season in his life. There was a time when his friends would say let's go throw the football or go trail bike riding or build a tree-house and the days of going swimming at the "Cliffs" where not many people went to when he was young, where they would swing on ropes far out over the edge of the ten-foot cliff and drop into the deep waters below. There were just things you outgrow no matter how much fun it was at the time, and back then we would run.

His thoughts drifted back to that time long ago when he was still a child. He thought of his father every day or so. The images of his face were still shots in his mind now, usually they were outside and dad would be smiling at him but there was also the lasting picture-perfect image of his father's dead face as he lay in a coffin. At any age this would be heartbreaking but at nine it was life-altering. Then a good friend of his, his same age, died when he was thirteen and he saw him in a coffin as well. It really made him start paying attention to things more and to being careful. It taught him how frail we are and we shouldn't throw caution totally to the wind by deliberately being reckless and careless. At thirteen he was still recovering from breaking his femur while playing sandlot football the year before. The pain was excruciating and it took nearly a year for him to get his strength partially back. He struggled to overcome his fear of getting hurt again by being overly cautious and gradually building his strength and courage back up again. He lived in the country, so to get his strength back he played in the woods, swung on vines across creeks and gullies, swam in the river and climbed trees, rode trail bikes and crazy ass untrained horses. His family had no money but when you lived in the country, where he lived; the forest was your playground and the river was nearby for fishing or swimming. There was still plenty to do and places to play, but as he got older, he became the cautious one in the group. Memories of the pain he suffered was what lingered in his mind. The muscle cramps inside his cast around the broken area of the bone were awful and he remembered screaming out at night when he was dreaming he was running or something and jerk his leg and a cramp would hit it. Oh my! He remembered that pain and those memories held him back from doing some of the riskier things he saw others do like bungee jumping or rock climbing. It cost him years in gaining his confidence back. Brad decided it was easy to be brave if you've never experienced level ten pain before. Emergency room nurses ask, "On a scale of one to ten, ten being the worst, how would you rate your pain right now? They should add, "level ten would be like being ripped apart by a sea monster." Then he added as if he were talking to Candy, "What number would you assign your pain level on a scale of one to ten, ten being the highest? I'm guessing ten." Brad always thought his broken leg deserved a ten rating but now he wanted to change it from ten to maybe a six. Even now he had to admit that the memories of that intense pain and the fear of ever feeling that pain again stayed with him always and gave rise to a kind of sixth sense alertness and awareness of his surroundings that has helped him recognize and avoid most dangerous situations. He used to think he could manage his fear this way but after seeing what happened to Candy, he wasn't sure of anything anymore.

His mind dwelled back to her often and his freshly-crushed heart had not stopped aching. Her tragic demise and his memories were etched in his mind's eye. He really wasn't in the mood to even think about doing anything right now.

Thoughts of Candy always brought his mind back to what had consumed him since all this happened, that there are giant sea monsters out there and he was afraid they were many more than we would ever know. He wanted to raise the alarm and tell everybody but he didn't think anyone would believe him or take him seriously, after all he wasn't even a real fisherman, he was just a survivor of a vicious attack that killed his fiancé and now most likely suffers from PTSD. He was a novice at best and he knew that he got lucky on his meeting with Wuss. What in the world could he do about giant squids or any other kind of sea creature? Who could he tell what he believed about these monsters? Who would care or listen? He knew he didn't really know the first thing about this sort of thing and he had no proof so he tried to put it out of his mind.

CHAPTER 13

In St. Petersburg, FL, Crystal Brook was proof-reading one of her own stories and preparing it for print. She finished her copy on some alligators that had invaded a local park pond when the image of the alligator's tail reminded her again of Wuss. When she finished her story she Googled, Wuss the giant sea monster and sure enough there he was all laid out on the morgue floor just where she saw him last. He was huge, 32 feet long, making the coroner standing beside it six times smaller. She thought of Brad and how he had to fight this monster to survive.

She had been trying to find other interesting stories but none lately captured her interest as much as this one. She was consumed by thoughts of Wuss, the giant squid and Brad Reno. She wanted to see Brad again, to see how he was doing and maybe get enough material to do a follow up story on Wuss. This was her story and she was hooked on it and on Brad Reno. She didn't believe he was the man he claimed to be. She had thought a lot about him and believed she was starting to understand him now. She was an expert at reading people but Brad was an enigma. She wanted to talk to him again, so, every time there was a story related to the ocean, the beach or boating in general she was always the first on the scene wanting to find out what the story was. Really, she was looking for a tie-in for a follow-up story about Wuss and a reason to talk to Brad.

Today when she checked her e-mail, there was one from Dr. Marshall England, Director of Research at UC San Diego. It read.

Marshall England
Dean of School of Marine Biology
University of California, San Diego, CA

Dear Ms. Brook, I am reaching out to you regarding your story on the colossal squid encounter of Mr. Brad Reno and the late, Ms. Candace Cotton.

As you may know, UC San Diego has an expanding research department. It is heavily involved with marine research and currently has ongoing projects in San Diego as well as the Alta Sea Research Center in Los Angeles.

He included a link to the facility. She had never heard of it so she clicked on the link. Her screen changed to a bright underwater view from a scuba diving camera holder's perspective, swimming along videoing everything in front of him and another diver. The scuba diver's video showed a picturesque view of a coral reef thriving with colorful fish of all sorts swimming in a crystal blue sea and a very active seabed full of flourishing sea life. Then she moved on to the facility itself. More beautiful, panoramic pictures of the dock area and videos went into great detail of the facilities capabilities and the mission statement that included, "to inspire innovation and exploration". She was impressed with the advances in aquaculture and its mission to provide an expanding area for agriculture for the future. They are professionals and educators looking for solutions to solving food shortage problems for generations to come by learning to grow and harvest safe, healthy foods. Currently they are finding ways to reduce the pressures on our current wild fishery system to keep up with demand. The area of the Alta Sea facility center included a 35-acre campus and deep-water access.

Links to many stories on the website discussed other missions and long-term goals in detail and the assets of Alta Sea that opened in 2013. It described itself as a research and port facility built right on City Dock No. 1, inside the Port of Los Angeles, its focus is mainly marine research of all kinds including exploration and innovation. It has research vessels including remote control drones with fully operational cameras and other recording devices with videos included. Another article included a picture of a submersible outfitted with state-of-the art equipment for marine scientific study and related matters. The port facility also has a fully operational aquarium with circulating sea water equipped with marine life support systems. Endangered sea animals from sickness, injury or for most any reason can be brought here for observation or treatment if needed. Post graduate and continuing education courses are given in fully functional classrooms. Marine scientist and other professionals, students and members of the community can meet, study, and share ideas together. It claims to have as its focus, the goal to leave the next generation a more sustainable ocean.

Crystal closed the article and went back to Dr. Marshall's email. He continued, UC San Diego has various studies ongoing, some by our staff and others have sponsors. One newly funded study among them has been to investigate the cause of a reduced fish population in a specific fishing area off the Southern California coast. They want to see if we can put a team together who can explain it. One area they have authorized us to explore is to see if there is a significant increase in Humboldt squid activity in this same area. What is of particular interest to members of our group at this time is the remarkable change in observable behavior of these creatures. We have a lot of questions for example, is there a correlation in the reduced fish population and the emergence or increase in the squid population? We don't know but the economic impact of having less fish in the local markets has severely hurt this community that depends heavily on the fishing industry. The survival of the local seafood market may depend on finding an answer. In comparison to last years' catch, the amount of local seafood being hauled in from this same area has dropped substantially, now exceeding sixty percent.

So, here's the bottom line. The fishermen believe the increased squid activity has frightened away the fish, add to that, there are many complaints of squids becoming tangled in netting causing excessive cost and down time. Some fishermen have moved to other areas of the coast and have stopped fishing in this area all together. We have been asked to look into it. I am reaching out to you as a resource for information in hopes that my team and I get the chance talk to you and Mr. Reno in the near future. I am including more attachments of recent news articles to assure you that this is a growing concern.

Article one had the headline: A record 12 feet long Humboldt squid caught by local fisherman now resides at the Alta Sea Water Aquarium. Picture included.

It detailed the plight of a local fisherman who caught an aggressive record length Humboldt squid in his fishing net off the coast of Baja, California. It measured 12 feet long and had hundreds of suction cups on its eight appendages and an eye that measured 10 inches across. What made it astonishing was that the average size of a Humboldt squid is about seven feet.

Dr. England added a note to this article. In it he explained that recent stories like this one and others, including Wuss, had already convinced him that it was time for a serious investigation into our local squid population. He explained how he had unsuccessfully petitioned the school for funding several times since he became department head but there was never even any debate before he was turned down for lack of community interest and sponsorship. Then help came from an unexpected source. Local fishermen started showing up at government offices asking for help and some came to his office for advice with stories and pictures of empty nets. One thing they were catching more and more of were large squids. Many of these squids were as small as a foot but others exceeded seven feet. The fishermen all were bothered by their voracity as they tried to escape their nets, cutting them to shreds. It was always amazing to listen to witnesses describe what they saw as they watched the slimy creature up close. The crew would complain that you could barely get near them without them wrapping their tentacles around everything they touched and some lashed out in forceful aggressive attacks.

He went on to say, with these eyewitnesses as new ammunition, he finally was able to get approval for funding and agreed to get it started. It was his charge to plan and oversee the project. To do this he began choosing his team, planning the plan and implementing the plan. His first objective was to stay focused and state the mission. If he was going to do it, it would be to further scientific knowledge. He would need help, including scientists with different disciplines and interest and backgrounds and perspectives. People with first-hand knowledge of these creatures would be most helpful as well as those crew members with experience who know how to respond in case of attack. He needed a team of experienced scientist, engineers, investigators and most importantly an experienced crew.

He included another attachment here which was an article published by NOAA discussing the work their research department was doing under a federal government grant. The article describes an area where an oil tanker had gone down ten years earlier off the Baja Peninsula. NOAA had been studying the effects of contaminates from this wreck on the local seafood market since then including the different species and quantities of sea life found in this area. Of key importance was that an enormous population of Humboldt squids have inhabited this area as well and their increased aggressiveness has been observed and documented. In a combined effort to find answers, UC San Diego Marine Department received additional funding for more staff and resources to also study the squids in this area. His department is now authorized and fully funded and staffed for this project.

Links to other stories included one of a child possibly being pulled off a small fishing boat by a large squid off the coast in Ixtapa, Mexico. Another story was about a local fisherman whose death was now being blamed on possibly a giant squid after being mistaken at first as a great white shark attack. There were precise images of the wounds of this attack victim. Crystal saw something familiar in the shape of the wounds and she wanted Brad to see them.

Crystal, being a good observer of human behavior, recognized a change in Dr. England's typing style. He was staccato at first, straight to the point, sell the idea, and talk them into coming. But now his typing seemed more thoughtful and deliberate. It seemed like he was slowing down and thinking deeper as he typed like he was giving her a class on what he was observing from his perspective. As she read, she tried to imagine the thought process of a curious man or woman posed with this problem. Where would they start; a curious scientist or a curious squid scientist. What questions would they be asking? Maybe he's developing an idea now, concentrating; just trying to think of everything that might give a clue to the missing fish problem or the increased squid's problem. Maybe he was tired from a long day. It seemed like his educated mind was working, wandering off in some un-explored direction even at this very moment. His desire to make her understand what he was up against in this e-mail showed to Crystal a sincere interest in finding answers to his questions. That's good, Crystal thought, he's a scientist, he should be curious. She wondered if he had ever suffered from attention deficit disorder, though. He went on to explain his areas of interest, one being the twelve-foot-long squid in captivity, he noted that most of these squids rarely grew larger than seven feet, so having one twelve feet long, she could tell he was excited to have access to study something he didn't know existed before. This was something new. He went on to say if they were fortunate enough to see another one of these oversized squids, he wanted to be prepared to document it in its entirety. They would attempt to photograph it, observe and record its physical features, its hunting and feeding habits and whatever else they could learn about it in the short time they were there in its habitat. They would then compare it to the one now in captivity. They would be interviewing other witnesses and looking for differences and similarities of their encounters to help determine as close as they could any behavioral differences. He also wanted to try to determine if they were concentrated in this area for a reason or will they migrate as they decimate the sea-life in an area. It had been previously established that the Humboldt squid hide in the deepest waters during daylight hours and only come to the surface at night. The ones encountered in these articles all occurred during the day. The average size of a Humboldt is seven feet long and hardly ever exceeds nine feet but the one in captivity is twelve feet long. That could mean that it's a different species all together or maybe they grow bigger than we thought. Now it's been documented that they have begun aggressively seeking out and attacking humans. It was very important that we have one to study in captivity while we gather more information to determine the reason for this newly observed behavior.

Dr. England forwarded all these stories to Crystal for her perusal and closed by saying that he and others have been concerned with this species of squid for years but we have been unable to get funding for a complete study until now. The pieces have fallen into place and we would like to do a thorough investigation. We are interested in asking you and Mr. Reno for your help, we have a few questions regarding your observations. Our students are mostly science majors looking for something new all the time. Finding answers to questions that haven't been thought of yet is what we are looking for. This is of particular interest because there are so many unanswered questions. One that comes to mind that a student recently asked was if there were any similarities in behavior of these squids and the one named, Wuss. We thought it might be a good idea to ask you.

The letter closed with the invitation. If she and Mr. Reno were available, there was funding to cover expenses for you both to be a part of the next planning meeting. There is a lot to learn about this species. We would be honored if you would join us in our effort

Marshall

After she finished Dr. England's e-mail, she conceded that his argument was compelling with sound and factually solid evidence and that he could be quite persuasive. It was no wonder he was able to get funding for what could turn out to be a large undertaking. She began thinking about what she had to do before she could go out of town for several days. After a moment she decided that she would make it work and wasted no time in putting together another e-mail and sending it to Brad.

Later that day, Brad finally got around to opening his e-mail. He was surprised when he saw a familiar name he hadn't heard from recently, Crystal Brook, Reporter WPBG, St. Petersburg, FL.

The e-mail read:

Hi stranger,
 I had hoped to hear from you by now... lol! You could say that I have ulterior motives for e-mailing you. You know me, always the reporter, but I also have been wondering how you were doing. Anyway, the other reason I'm reaching out to you is that I received a request from the Dean of Marine Studies at UC San Diego. I wanted you to see it. He included some attachments. I especially wanted you to see the pictures from this one story specifically about a squid attack off the coast of Mexico. I attached a better picture. Tell me if anything stands out to you.
Crystal

Brad opened the first of several attachments and saw the referenced documents. He read about the incident where the fisherman was attacked and when he saw the picture, he hesitated and looked closer. He tried to get an idea of the size of this scar. It was not unusual for there to be shark attacks in that part of the ocean. He had seen pictures in the news from helicopters flying over the beaches of Southern California and videoing large great white sharks just a few yards farther out than swimmers.

One article talked about the family of a child in Mexico that was distraught and beside themselves with anguish since they went boating last month. Their child was on the boat with a life jacket on, the next moment the child was gone. They believed he was dragged over the side and he completely disappeared. The life jacket was worthless and the body has never been found. The parents said they believe something pulled their son out of the boat because he had been sitting still and had not said anything and there was no way he could have climbed up over the side without someone noticing him up and moving around. Something took him, they just knew it. There was a slimy residue and fishy stench left behind as well. They could not find anyone willing to help them find answers. Brad felt bad for the parents, "So now we know what not having money or power gets you during a tragedy. Nothing!" he said out loud, now he felt bad and was more curious at the same time.

Another article was from an incident that happened off the California coast just a few days ago. The headline read, "Another Wuss? Perhaps" The man-eating colossal squid named Wuss that was caught by Florida fisherman, Brad Reno from Charleston, SC, was back in the news on Thursday. Mauricio Lopez, a shrimp boat captain, reported that a crew member was picked up and dragged off his boat by an incredible sight. A large pale snake-like arm came over the side of his shrimp trawler and as soon as it touched the first person it came to, it wrapped around him and snatched him over the side in the blink of an eye. The closest crew member to him witnessed this happen and ran to the side just in time to see a turbulent disturbance in the waters about ten or so feet from the trawler. He promptly yelled, "Man overboard!" alerting the rest of the crew, then he grabbed a life preserver attached to a long line and ran back to the side. He saw his shipmate come to the surface and he bravely risked his own life by jumping into the water to help his mate get the life preserver around him. The two of them were then pulled in by other crew members but unfortunately the fisherman who was grabbed and pulled over the side did not survive his injuries. He was pronounced dead on the scene by the boat's captain.

Brad read it again. When he came to the description of his injuries and cause of death, the coroner had explained the cause of death was most likely drowning with subsequent traumatic limb amputation and multiple deep and shallower lacerations causing extreme blood loss which would be congruent with injuries that one would expect to be sustained from an extended attack by a large shark, perhaps a great white but he couldn't rule out that a giant squid could also have caused these types of injuries.

Finding water in his lungs would explain the drowning as the cause of death and that's what really scared Brad. He realized that this man's death was not immediate and it had to be terrifying and excruciatingly painful, then he froze when he read the next part. Here was the picture Crystal had sent. It was a partially circular bite wound with a violent soft tissue tear around the circle which the coroner had made note of because it looked out of place. He lifted his shirt to see if he could still make out the scar on his side where Wuss got his suction cup on his skin. It looked the same except his wound was substantially smaller. The coroner had no explanation other than an odd bite pattern with extensive tissue trauma and only chose to leave the possibility of it being a giant squid mark because he had only recently been looking at the pictures from the autopsy of Wuss. This one wound clearly matched the pattern a scientist might expect from a large suction cup and jagged laceration from a giant squid but it would be impossible to reach a definite conclusion with that scant evidence...still.

Crystal also attached a picture of an ancient yellowed map of the Earth and seas and an article below it tagged. When he enlarged it, he quickly saw in one area an artist's rendition of a sea monster. It looked like a giant octopus but the artist considered it to be a prehistoric sea monster. It was the kind illustrators used to draw on maps to indicate unexplored regions of Earth where it was believed these ancient underwater monsters hid. All sailors and pirates knew the old wooden sailing ships were no match for such a creature so only the bravest men signed on, but only then for the promises of shared booty would they be willing to face their greatest fears. There was only one goal for a pirate, to get the chance at what they considered life's great rewards, fame and fortune and maybe take a few lives in the process. "Arrr matey! I'd like to see you take on one of these bloody creatures from the depths of the sea." Brad finished.

The last article dated almost two years ago was titled, "Squid Squad Attacks the UC Scientific Submersible"

This one included a picture of a bright yellow damaged two-man submersible being held up above the deck of the UC research ship like a trophy sailfish. It belonged to the University of California and was hauled out of the water after being briefly out of touch with the research ship and carried on a turbulent ride during an attack by a squad of what was determined to be Humboldt squids. It is uncertain what provoked the attack, but what is certain is the aggressive nature of these sea creatures. Dr. Marshall England and Dr. Bud Martin, pictured here standing together near the submersible, were aboard the sub when it was attacked. During a joint press briefing, both scientists agreed the attack came totally by surprise and the speed with which the squids moved and the viciousness of the squad that attacked them was incredible. "Easily" Dr. England stated, "as fast as a shark grabs a fish." At one point, the article stated, a large squid came out of nowhere, quite possibly exceeded eight feet long and intentionally and forcefully collided with their sub with what could only be described as a deliberate collision to do damage. Dr. Martin stated, He thought it was over for them and their sub when they lost control and were headed down. The article described in detail what the scientist witnessed. Dr. Martin stated that, "The entire submarine felt like a huge boulder fell on top of them. It made a dent they could see on the inside wall." The scientist then sounded less scholarly with Dr. Martin's description of what happened next. The quote went, "We went spinning wildly briefly, like a big old yellow top, when it wrapped its tentacles around the sub damaging the rudder. That's when we both knew what it was and in a split second we were solidly in its grasp. It carried us over a natural drop-off beside where a wreck lay into much deeper waters in a handful of seconds." They both described the feeling of the pressures building quickly as it went deeper. "Then, after about thirty seconds, it released us and we came back to the surface about two hundred meters from where we went down. Once on the surface, we were able to reestablish contact with our ship and were retrieved." Because of the mission of the crew, the sub was equipped with cameras for scientific exploration inside and mounted on the hull. The cameras mounted outside were all destroyed but from the inside cameras, a few good pictures came out. The article ended with the statement that the incident was being investigated. Brad wondered what that meant.

The story that followed the interview began by identifying the location as off the coast of Baja California and described in detail, the incredible story told in a sensational way and included the very limited video of the expedition via submersible to explore this area which lay about 30 miles off the mainland. The UC Research Group had been routinely studying this area for years without incident, measuring the oil content of the water and soil in a large older oil slick area. The study included taking copious pictures of the emerging life around the area. Its location was near the edge of a drop-off;

which in itself created a whole new line of questioning about the sea life that comes from the deeper waters to find food in shallower waters. Nocturnal habits around the contaminated area were also being observed and recorded and collecting samples of sea life were part of the study. Levels of inorganic contaminates that are being consumed by these animals can yield valuable data. This information aids in determining the quality and quantity of fishing as well as informing the local fishermen areas they should avoid.

The article included a photograph of where a suction cup from the creature had attached to one of the portholes. One of the scientists was able to keep his head and measure it as it spread out on the glass. He gave an estimate of the squid's size of greater than seven feet.

Brad finished the article and replied to Crystal's message.

Brad emailed:

> I read about the circular pattern with the lacerations inside, I don't know what to say. I'll get back to you. By the way, it was nice to see your name pop-up on my e-mail. I know how busy you are.
> Brad.

Then he went to back to the article about the fisherman and started reading it again from the beginning. He was only partly surprised by this story. He had great suspicions that there were plenty of giant squids or squads of giant squids; however how you want to say it, they were out there in the deep waters. He knew immediately that the wound described by the coroner on the shark attack victim may have been another giant squid attack. He was fairly certain that at least one of those marks was caused by a giant squid and sharks don't reach into large boats and pull people off but he knew for certain that giant squids do. Where was he? San Diego? All of a sudden, it hit him. The population of these monsters could be growing and their feeding areas expanding faster than he imagined.

He was finishing up with this e-mail when another came in from Crystal.

Brad
   I'm not so busy. Well, I am a little bit...maybe. Lol! Okay, I do have another reason to be e-mailing you.
   Dr. England, who is the department head, has asked to interview you and me about Wuss and he said if I wanted to, he would agree to me writing a story to go along with their scientific observations for my readers that I can have published. His group of researchers believes they have evidence of more giant squids or maybe a different species. They were interested in the story of your encounter with Wuss and they invited us to come and discuss our experience to better prepare them for their next expedition into this area again. They wanted me to reach out to you with the invitation. Call me.
Crystal

She left her phone number at the bottom of the e-mail. Brad studied it for a long time. He wasn't sure why but a surge of adrenaline rushed through his body leaving him feeling anxious like a heavy burden was placed on his shoulders. Maybe it was too much coffee but now he felt nauseated. A flashback of Candy standing on the deck just before Wuss took her away was still fresh in his mind. He wasn't ready now and didn't expect to ever be ready to see something like that again.

It had to be a coincidence that Crystal contacted him just as he was thinking about this. He had been pondering the question of who could he tell about his theory of the ever-growing population of these giants and how dangerous they could become and he gets this e-mail from Crystal. He decided right then he was not thrilled about seeing another one.

Brad e-mailed back,

Dearest Crystal,
  I have been concerned that these creatures were not being investigated. I do have questions as well but after thinking further about it, I have decided that I am not interested in ever seeing one of these again but I am glad someone is taking a serious look at them now.
Brad

Brad looked at the number. He put his phone down and went to the fridge. He grabbed a Diet Mountain

Dew and popped the tab. He walked back to pick up his phone and carried it and his drink outside to the deck overlooking the saw-grass bordering the inter-coastal waterway. He was thinking it through a little more and decided there was a way he could help. Maybe he could talk to them over Skype or something; surely he didn't need to be there. He decided that would be his answer and then maybe ask her to dinner sometime in the future, "Yes, that's the ticket" he repeated the old Jon Lovitz line from his, "Liar" skit. He picked up his phone and typed in the number. It rang once and he heard her voice on the other end. "Brad!" she said excitedly, "I'm so glad you changed your mind. We have a lot to talk about." "Hello, Crystal. It's nice to hear your voice," Brad returned the compliment. "Brad, I am so excited. Dr. England thinks they may have found another giant squid. They want us to come out there, Brad, both of us." Brad jumped in right here, "Whoa, Speedy, you're way ahead of me." Brad told her his idea of a simple phone call on Skype and it will be all done and everyone will get what they want. There was a moment of silence on the other end.

"Brad, I want you to come, please." Brad at that moment decided he wouldn't ask her out. "I'm sorry Candy, I can't make it." Crystal caught the mistake but didn't mention it. Brad caught it too, "I'm sorry, I meant Crystal". "It's okay, Brad," She paused. "Can I come see you? I'll buy you dinner on my expense account." "If you want to, that would be fine," he answered. "Great, can you meet me at the Charleston airport Marriott on

Friday?" she asked. "Sure," he said. "Great, I'll e-mail you a time once I make reservations." she said. Then Brad replied, "That will be fine, Crystal."

After he hung up, he felt sick. He thought he wanted to see her again but now he wasn't sure. He wasn't happy or excited like he thought he would be. Instead, he felt sad that he wasn't more excited about the proposition. His anxiety level was very high and he was shaking like he had two cups of coffee. He wasn't really interested in talking to anybody. He sat on his deck and watched a blue heron walking up and down the edge of the creek looking into the water, searching for a meal of his own. He thought about calling her back or better yet, just texting her that he decided he wasn't ready to talk about it but decided not to overreact. He tried to stop thinking about it. In a little while, she texted him to meet her at the hotel at 5 o'clock tomorrow, Friday. He said he would.

That evening he began thinking about why Crystal was coming. What if she started pressuring him to go? He hoped she would accept his answer but suspected it wasn't going to be easy. He would have to steer her back to the Skype idea if she persisted. Maybe, she wanted to say that she would like to get to know him better personally? He shrugged that thought off. He wasn't really interested but he wished he was, how traumatized was he? The next day came and Brad was feeling only slightly better about meeting her. He began getting ready for dinner at three and felt a headache coming on. Crystal had texted him that her flight was on time and she would be ready at six.

When he got to the hotel, he called her from the lobby. She invited him up to her room so they could talk. When she opened the door, he only then remembered how beautiful she was. "Hi! Come in," she said excitedly. "Hi," he said and slowly walked in. She surprised him with a cordial kiss on the cheek. Her perfume was very nice. "Come in and have a seat." "Okay," he said and added, "you look great, and I like your perfume." "Thank you," she smiled and said he looked great too but he wasn't feeling it. He sat down in a straight-backed chair at the table next to the window. He glanced out the window to distant lights on the busy runways, some red, others white and green, some flashing and others stayed on. Airplanes were visible on the tarmac, moving along the runways and at the terminals. He lingered at the comings and goings long enough for Crystal to start the conversation as she handed him an ice-cold Corona.

"Brad, I think it would do us both good to get away for a few days. I want to go but I want you to go with me." "Oh Crystal, you don't need me to tag along," he said. "There isn't much I can add and it would just be a big waste of money for me to come." "No, it wouldn't Brad. I already have your ticket approved and by the way, my editor wants you to go too so you can look after me," she smiled. "You can be my protector." "Protector?" he responded, "Yes, well, I didn't do such a great job last time." She knew he was referring to Candy. "That wasn't your fault," she countered. "You are a courageous man Brad Reno and I want you to go with me." "Well, it didn't take courage to stand there," he added. "The courage came later," she continued, "when you chose to stay out there." Crystal saw the painful memories in Brad's expression. "I didn't really do anything but stand there," he said again. "She was swept right overboard... by this thing," Brad went on unable to shut his own mouth. "I did nothing to stop it. One second she was there and I was there and we were looking at this crazy thing and then, while she still had the look of a child's amazement...a child's amazement" he accentuated to illustrate how quick everything happened, "on her face from watching the fish jumping around and the next thing I see is this giant tentacle coming out of nowhere and landing between me and her; and her look, her expression. Her look of wonder turned to mouth dropping, wide-eyed amazement and that turned to fear right in front of me and total shocking surprise, and her scream was cut off to a dead silence in an instant," he took a breath. "So, you couldn't do anything, Brad. What could you have done?" He went on, "She knew immediately she was in trouble and it happened so fast," he stopped. "I'm sorry, I should be quiet," he finished. Crystal saw the pain in his eyes and said softly, "You brought her home Brad. What is it the Rangers say? No man left behind. That's you Brad, you couldn't leave her behind. You brought her home.....to her family. You brought closure the only way you could. You don't even know what you did Brad, do you?" she asked rhetorically, "or what it meant to others. Do you know that nearly everyone I've talked to about this story views you as a very brave man but not for the reason you might think." Brad heard her voice begin to crack and looked up at her. "Just imagine if you had not done what you did. Just think of the void that would have been left behind. The not knowing what happened, the unanswered questions and suspicion and investigation and a multitude of interviews with elaborate, critical news stories and accusations." She saw Brad's eyes were floating in tears yet to fall. She felt the conversation getting heavy again and a solemn look was starting to consume him so she tried to think of something to snap him out of it. She said, "Heck, me alone...I would have pestered the police to investigate you for suspicion of murder or something." Brad looked up at her, "Really?" he asked. "What?" she asked back, "I'm a reporter and I have questions when people just fall off stopped boats never to be seen again," then she gave him a challenging raised eyebrows look, he gave her a sad look back. "Brad you were courageous for staying there. It took courage to stay. You made a deliberate decision to stay and that made the biggest difference of all. See Brad, I told you I can read people so let me explain to you what I read in what you did," Crystal began. Brad jumped in, "In all honesty I don't remember what I was thinking but I do remember I was drinking."

Crystal smiling said, "That's okay too. I would have had one with you if I had been there." Brad started thinking to himself about Candy's religion again.

Crystal saw his look become lost in something that deeply bothered him but he didn't speak. He was thinking how Candy didn't have time to repent, she didn't have time to say, Oh, Jesus! or Oh, crap! She barely had time to scream. To regain his attention, she went a little further to draw him out of his deep sadness. "As a matter of fact, I think I would have liked to have seen that fight. I bet you were something to see!" she added with a sense of awe. "Yes. Whatever you are thinking I bet I was something else, like cowed down in the cabin," Brad replied and he let out a little laugh. Crystal heard his little anxiety filled laugh and this made a smile pop-up on her own face. She hoped she made him feel better. He was a good guy and she liked him. Brad went on, "I'm just glad there were no sharks around. When I think about how long I was in that water and Wuss was right beside me it would seem like a tempting meal for a passing shark."

"Hmmm," Crystal thought about it for a few seconds then she said, "I know you weren't cowed down in the cabin because I saw a giant squid with a paddle oar stuck in its eye," Brad smiled a little and jumped in, "A paddle oar? Well saying it like that's not going to win you any Pulitzer. You're a writer you need to embellish it just a little to capture the moment," he said a little sarcastically in light fun. Crystal went on, "and do you think a shark would swim around in an area where something like that lived?" Brad paused at that notion. "To be honest with you, that thought never crossed my mind," he reflected back to then, "I wish I had thought of that actually, maybe I would have been less terrified in the water," he confessed thinking back, unable to even remember the level of fear he felt in his recollection. "There was no way you could know for sure," this time she conceded. She looked at him and could tell he was feeling better.

Brad began his quickly prepared excuse in a calm voice, totally in control. "I told you I was afraid of that thing and now you're asking me to do what? I know they are not going to kill it if they find one, so what are they going to do, try to catch it?" "No," Crystal quickly inserted, "they're not going to try to catch it, they're just going to see if it's around there and observe it and tag it if possible. Maybe get a chance of filming one. They have a little mini sub with several cameras mounted on it." "That wouldn't be prudent," Brad responded, "I already saw what they did to the other one." "Awww, come on Brad. You get an all-expense paid trip to Southern California with me," she added with a smile as if that was a bonus, with the hope he would come with her to investigate and talk to these guys. "They're eager to meet you," she added.

"No thanks, Crystal. I never want to even look over the side of a boat again." "I don't believe that, Brad," Crystal challenged. " "What do you mean? You don't believe what? I told you I was frightened to death during that entire time," Brad went on. "So, you say," she feigned skepticism and Brad's eyebrows went up. "What? You don't believe me? That's not something a guy can easily admit to, you know," he confessed.

Crystal persisted, "I don't believe you were frightened, Brad." "Oh yes I was!" he argued back. "I think you were upset. I think you were mad," "Oh yes," Brad blurted. Crystal went on, "hurt, angry, nervous," "Yes, all that," he gave her that too. "And maybe a little apprehensive because you didn't know what was going to happen next or when?" "You are right about that," he conceded. "And don't forget scared," he reiterated. "Really?" She countered. "I'm sure of it," he said again. "I still don't believe you. I'll tell you what you are. You're a big fat liar!" she scolded him. "Well, I wasn't expecting that," he responded to her cutting criticism. "I'm sorry but I don't believe you because of something else you said. Want to know what it was?" she asked. "I don't care what you say, I'm not listening," Brad countered. "You said you couldn't leave, Brad, because you couldn't leave Candy behind. Do you remember saying that? Was that true?" she stopped talking. "Yeah," Brad confirmed in a low voice. "No, you weren't afraid, Brad. If you had been afraid, you would have left, no, you would have torn out of there wide open as fast as you could. You would have run away...but you stayed... and that took courage." "I did have beers left," Brad sparred back. "That's okay, that still makes you the bravest man I've ever met," she stopped talking again and Brad looked at her. This time she was smiling at him but at the same time he saw tears in her eyes. To break the silence Brad said, "Give me a few more excuses and I'll write a book and title it, What Happened," Brad said. "Nope, you can't, that name has already been taken but I'll tell YOU what happened." she chided him back. Brad was shocked by what he was hearing. "It wasn't courage either," he finished. "I don't care what you say, Brad Reno. I know better and I want you to go with me. Be my, protector." "Boy did you pick the wrong guy," he said. "I don't think so," she countered. Crystal was feeling confident in her assessment now. "I don't think so at all. And you can say you stayed because you loved her or not, I don't believe that either and I'll tell you why. It's because that's who you are, Brad Reno. It took me a while to figure you out because you are rare. You are not typical," she smiled as she said this, "You have a rare trait. That's why I didn't see it at first. Remember the first time we met, I was skeptical of you but I'm an expert at finding out people's motives for doing things or like in your case, not doing something. I got you figured out, Mr. Liar." She smiled as she said that last part. "I know a few things, Brad. I know you never saw anything like Wuss before. I know that and I suspect Wuss had never encountered anything like you." "No, probably not," Brad said as he looked up. "I know you were there over twenty-four hours after the attack, so not only were you not afraid, you were defiant." Brad jumped in, "I was not!" he fired back like it was a bad thing. Crystal cut him off. "You named it, Wuss, sorry, but that sounds defiant to me. I don't believe you intended on leaving that spot and you would have died there if the Coast Guard had not found you. I believe you would have stayed not just because it was Candy but because you would have done that for anyone." "I don't know about that", Brad returned her rebuttal. "Really Brad, who? Who would you have left out there and not tried to save or retrieve or find proof of what happened to them? Who Brad? Anybody else? Me? I don't think so, nor anyone else. That's not who you are Brad Reno. I'm sure you might have had a lot of things going on inside of you but fear wasn't one of them." "Lawyers, I maybe would have left lawyers," Brad finished. "Of course, lawyers, they don't count," Crystal smiled. "I guess not," he agreed, "But I really, really didn't like it!" and with that he closed his argument. "I know," she said softly. He solemnly looked up into her eyes and asked, "You think I'm fat?" he asked. "No," she smiled.

"Okay", Brad said. "Okay, what?" she asked. "Okay, I'll go. I guess I'll go, like the song says." "What song?" Crystal asked. "The 'should I stay or should I go' song. You know, If I stay there could be trouble if I go it could be double." "That's true," Crystal said. "That's not funny," Brad replied. "Anyway," Crystal added, "that's good because I already got us two tickets to San Diego, leaving Sunday at noon. We should arrive with the time change about 3 or 4 in the afternoon." Brad was speechless. "Brad? Did I lose you? Brad? Say something. You'll go with me, right?" "I'll go. What is it I'm supposed to do?" asked Brad. "I'll tell you over dinner. They didn't even serve a snack on the plane."

They walked down to the restaurant and the hostess seated them. Brad was impressed with the confidence Crystal exuded and the kindness she extended to others. Her smile disarmed even the most tired waitress and brought a smile to their face. They were seated when she pulled a copy of the list of things the scientists were curious about that Brad may be able to add some insight to. She handed it to Brad. "Dr. England, the head of the Research Department, sent me a letter outlining questions for you. You really don't have to give a proper lecture or anything it's more of an eyewitness account with as much detail as you want to reveal and they may have a few questions for you." He glanced at it and saw there were only a few questions there. Mostly, just about things he observed. He folded it up and put it in his shirt pocket. Then she handed him his ticket and boarding pass as she smiled. He tilted his head and looked into her eyes. "You were quite sure of yourself, weren't you?" he stated flatly. "I told you Brad, I got you figured out," and smiled her beautiful smile at him. He tried to match her gaze that was focused directly into his eyes but looked down after just a moment. She could tell he was concerned about her. "It'll be okay, Brad, I'll be there for you, too. See?" and she showed him her ticket. "I'm riding with you. I'm going to make sure you don't back out." His heart felt like it just melted inside of him and he felt tears welling up in his eyes. He tried to blink them away. No one had ever told him that they would, "be there for him," before. Their dinner was delicious and filling and the glass of wine made him tired. He still felt sad after everything so he said goodnight at the elevator. She felt his pain, touched his arm, kissed his cheek and said goodnight.

CHAPTER 14

Sunday morning, he got up early and packed light. Knowing he would only be there a couple of days, he only brought carry-on luggage. He found a spot in long term parking at the Charleston Airport and hopped a shuttle to the terminal. He had his ticket and boarding pass so he looked at the monitor and found his gate number, bypassed the Delta counter and proceeded to his gate where he was to meet up with Crystal and they would fly across country together. When he approached his gate, he didn't know if Crystal would be there yet but couldn't stop himself from looking, maybe hoping he would see her. He stopped and it only took a second to recognize her from 30 feet away in the crowded sitting area. She was looking closely at her phone, concentrating on something important it looked like. Her focus was complete and she was off in another world. "Wow," he said to himself when he saw her. She looked gorgeous even from where he was standing. She was dressed business casual in a pale gray skirt and a white blouse with red stripes and perfect makeup with matching bright red lipstick, her rich blond hair curled freely on her shoulders. She glanced up right at him like she could sense him watching and saw him as he was looking her way, that's when he saw her beautiful glacial blue eyes light up. He felt a warm wave flush through his body. It was nice to see someone smile at him again. He thought for a second that she genuinely looked happy to see him but he was sure it was just the excitement of the trip. He tried to smile back but his mind hadn't cleared from losing Candy yet. He felt a heaviness in his chest and an emptiness in his heart. He liked Crystal a lot though and he wanted to help her if he could.

Crystal put her phone away and got up to come meet him. "Hi Brad, it's so good to see you!" she said as she reached out and kissed his cheek. He twisted his mouth and managed a half kiss back. He did get a whiff of the perfume she was wearing. "You look great," he said, followed by, "you smell good, too." "Thank you," she said, still smiling. They sat down beside each other and Brad asked her how her job was going. She talked about a couple of stories she covered since he saw her. A tragic drive-by shooting nightmare was the latest one of hers that made national news, a real heart breaker. She asked Brad how his ribs were doing from his encounter with Wuss. He told her, his doctor said he was better now, even though he admitted he was still protective of them. They continued their conversation non-stop until boarding call.

Brad hadn't noticed before they boarded the plane

but now, he saw their seats were next to each other. He asked her if she wanted the aisle or the middle. She picked the aisle so he sat down first. A middle-age man in a casual opened collar Hawaiian shirt sat next to the window and was watching the happenings outside. After they were all situated and suitably comfortable in their seats for the moment, Brad asked her about this group he was going to meet. Brad started the conversation with a question. "Have you talked to anybody from the school since we talked?" "Yes," she said, "I told them we would be there tonight and can meet them tomorrow. They were glad you decided to come."

Brad didn't know much about Crystal except that she was good at what she did. She had a sixth sense about what made people tick and she could get to the truth quickly. Other than that, he didn't know much about her. "So, how did you get into this field? Did you always want to be a reporter?" he asked her. She wasn't sure how much she wanted to reveal about herself but she thought it might help Brad to understand that things hadn't been so easy for her either.

"It's a long story. I was married. I married my college sweetheart soon after graduation, the big college jock on campus of course, destined to be a great car salesman," she smiled. "We were happy for a while and I soon became pregnant," she paused here. Brad, who had been momentarily distracted by the attendant, turned back towards her and listened quietly. "We had a son, Jimmy, named after his father and grandfather." Brad caught the word, "had," he hoped he hadn't opened an old wound but she seemed to want to share this with him, so he sat quietly and listened. "He was a great little guy, full of smiles, just the sweetest little boy and his papa loved him so much. While I was out buying groceries and James was at work," she paused, "You see, Jimmy was not even three, he found his granddaddy's handgun under the edge of his bed," she couldn't go on. "It was horrible." Brad heard her voice crack. "I couldn't believe it. I got home and just as I was pulling into the driveway, James Sr. came running out of the house carrying this little blood-soaked bundle. I saw it was my little baby in his arms with blood all over them both. I heard sirens closing in fast and I just stood there beside my baby as he died." Brad didn't move as she shared with him the pain she had suffered. He felt so bad for her, he put his hand on hers and she left it there. "Afterwards, I really couldn't face James, who was always mad at me and blamed me for leaving Jimmy with Sr., but Sr. loved Jimmy and Jimmy loved his poppa. After a year, we decided it wasn't going to get better. He was gone more and more and said he didn't care about me anymore and told me to my face how he couldn't look at me without getting angry. I couldn't take it either just being around his family. The constant grieving from everyone was overwhelming. I was sinking into depression and I knew it. All I could think about was how it really was my fault for what happened." Brad stopped her there, "I don't think so." She went on, "I gave up trying and we separated. During the separation I decided I needed to go back to work. That's the reason I'm telling you this about me. I know how you feel. I know you feel to some degree responsible for what happened to Candy but you shouldn't, no more than I should feel responsible for what happened to Jimmy. Anyway, it was difficult smiling through interviews when all I wanted to do was lie down. I began to look for a job that I might actually like but figured I couldn't get anyway. I decided it was now or never to pursue my dream job of news reporter.

My degree was in English with a journalism minor. I took a speech class and signed up to the local Toastmasters and began speaking weekly in front of the group, like we do. Once I discussed things a little too close to home about my life and I didn't go back after that. Going there had helped though and to my amazement I felt better than I had in a long time. I decided to apply for work as a journalist at the places around town and wound up getting a job in the editing department at WPBG. I started filling in on weekends and fifteen years later, I'm still here. At the time though, I still delved too much in the past, couldn't sleep some nights, I was all alone and depression was just below the surface. I didn't know how to grieve. I wasn't sure I was doing it right. I didn't know how to behave being the mother who let her only child have access to a loaded gun. I felt guilty but didn't really know what to think. Sr. shouldn't have had his gun in a place James could get to. You would think you wouldn't have to tell another adult that, so I started to blame him more. It helped to spread out the blame. I had to find a way to save myself so I decided to focus on work."

"The first time I saw myself on TV, I realized how fat I was and I became obsessed with my weight. It had been over four years since I had been pregnant and was still fat, I could see it in the mirror. I knew I was competing for air time and image was important. I began to skip meals intentionally and if I had to eat in public, I would purge as soon as I could get back to my room or back home. I didn't care that it wasn't healthy and I was becoming a mess, I really didn't care what I did to myself, I was going to get back to a size four if it killed me. I began to lose weight, people at work noticed, men started talking to me more and inviting me to dinners. Then, I couldn't stop the dieting. I had totally lost my appetite. I had to make myself eat," she paused for a second. "One day James stopped by my office. I think he wanted to ask me out to dinner or something. Anyway, he saw a picture that I had framed and hung with other pictures on the wall at work along with my diploma and other things. It was of me and a guy from a work lunch meeting where we both received an award. I liked the picture but had no interest in the guy but of course James didn't believe me. We were already divorced. I don't know why but he became jealous when he saw how much weight I had lost. He got angry, called me every dirty degenerate name he could think of and then left. I became depressed again and more determined and swore I would get away from him. I felt that if I could just lose a few more pounds, I could wear the clothes that made me look perfect and I could get the job I wanted. I fainted one day on location at an industrial fire site of all places. I fell and gave myself a concussion and was taken to the hospital where my doctor told me my health was deteriorating. He said I was starving my body but of course I didn't believe it because I had textbook anorexia nervosa. They stood me in front of a full-length mirror and began showing me places on my bony body where I had nearly total muscle loss. My legs were skin and bones, my face was sunken in and I had terrible skin turgor on the backs of my hands," she pulled at the skin on the back of her hand to show Brad. He could see how thin and dehydrated her skin still was and her neck looked like you could wrap one hand completely around it. "My skin was dotted with pimples and I couldn't believe it was me. I was 40 but looked 60 so I became more depressed. I even believed I could still grab fat around my waist. It was getting close to Christmas that year and I was suffering through another depressing day like every day back then," She paused to gather her thoughts.

"Before the accident, James' family had all attended the same church and we continued going after we were married. Church was important to Sr. and now with his son and grandson beside him in the pew, he held his head high and accepted all the compliments that came his way with a big smile. He sang from the hymnal full-throated and listened obediently to the service. He tried to set a good example and hoped to make attending church a priority every Sunday and at Christmas, especially, the Christmas program and the Easter Sunrise Service, those were must attend services. After the accident, I stopped going for over a year but it didn't make me feel better so I knew that wasn't the answer. I was feeling particularly melancholy one Sunday morning a week or so before Christmas, when I was like that, it would always give me comfort to remember Jimmy and the smile on his face when I tried to kiss his neck. He would blush and hold his head down and scrunch up his shoulders because he was so ticklish. I started crying as usual and decided to get out of the house and go to church." Brad noticed that she smiled when she said his name.

"The church was having a Christmas service and some friends had invited me so I put on my size four dress and held my head up as best I could. I was talking to one my friends when I saw Sr. sitting a ways away. I didn't see James and I didn't recognize Sr. at first, he had aged and was thin, frail and sad. He was wearing a suit and tie and I remember it crossed my mind that if he laid down in a coffin right now and I closed it and buried it, I don't think he would object. My friend told me he had not missed a service since the accident. Then she told me this, "Sr. blames himself, James Jr. blames him too; so, I guess you do too." Then she said, "I can't blame any of you, it was a terrible accident but Sr. has never forgiven himself." I would occasionally glance the old man's way but never saw him smile. He looked so sad. I didn't speak to him then. I wasn't convinced he really cared how I felt. I thought he might just be looking for sympathy or pity but I had no pity for him. He was just an irresponsible, careless old man that allowed something unforgivable to happen and he wanted sympathy? I had no sympathy for him or my husband who sided with his daddy so he wouldn't get cut from his will but despises him all the while. I thought I knew them all and their motives but I was still full of anger and bitterness towards them all, anyway I went back the next Sunday," she picked back up the story, "and he was there so I kept going every week more to see if Sr. was there than for the service. It was April when I volunteered to help in the kitchen to prepare a meal. I turned a corner and nearly ran into Sr. He looked startled and almost afraid of me, like he was even afraid to look at me and he held his head down unable to meet my look eye to eye and he said, "Excuse me," like he didn't know who I was and was in a hurry. I didn't say anything. I continued to go to church on Sundays and every Sunday he was there."

The flight attendant brought some drinks by and they both got Diet Cokes. Crystal picked up where she left off. "One Sunday, the preacher, Father Gray, invited me to his office. He said he was worried for me. He didn't mention Sr. or my emaciated frame; he just asked if he could pray with me, so, I did. Afterwards, we walked into the dining area and had a small lunch together. I remember wanting to go throw up but there were too many people around and the urge passed. I decided that day to make myself stop trying to throw up. I was wearing my size four then and I had begun trying to eat healthy again, you know, small bites only and I tried never to fill up. I did put back on a little weight, anyway, I continued to go to church regularly and started noticing him less and less on Sundays. Then one evening almost a year later I attended the Christmas concert and I saw Sr.'s name on the program. To get him back involved with the church, Pastor Gray talked Sr. into participating in the Christmas play. He was playing the part of a wise man. At the end of the program the cast members were all standing in a row at the front of the church and the congregation filed past like they did every time for every occasion to thank them. As I was nearing Sr., I noticed him look toward me. As I got closer, his expression changed, it became strained and he was not happy at all to be standing there. As I came up to him, he turned white, took a step back and tripped or his legs buckled, anyway he sat hard on the floor. Those around him grabbed too late to catch him. As I reached down to help, I heard him, he was sobbing. He broke down right there, right then and was letting it all out. I asked him if he was okay. He tried to look up at me but he was a mess. The crowd was gathering around quickly to make themselves useful if they were needed for something. Anyway, a lot of us were there but he looked up at me, directly into my eyes this time and still crying, his face contorted and red, he said, "I'm sorry, Crystal. I'm so sorry. I'm so, so sorry," he kept repeating that and then said, he never would have done anything to hurt Jimmy. I told him that I knew that. That's when I started crying and sat down right beside him on the floor and he put his arms around my neck and cried uncontrollably for a little while. I guess it was helpful just to hear him accept some responsibility. We talked a little more after that, nothing serious and never about James Jr. or Jimmy again. I didn't go back to that church either. It was time to move on, so I started accepting travel assignments that no one else wanted and was given more air time which led to more assignments. I felt better and was able to function again. Last February, Sr. died. I don't know where James is anymore and I suppose I have to say I'm not the same person as before."

Brad noticed his hand was still on top of hers lying on the armrest between them. He felt sympathy toward her, a kinship, like survivors of a tragic event where there are multiple casualties and only a small number of survivors. They sometimes admit to feeling guilty for living, for being the one who walked away unscathed. It made some of them wonder if God has a greater purpose for them that they can't figure out while others become depressed simply because they survived when others didn't. He supposed Crystal may feel that way, he knew he felt that way at times himself about Candy's premature demise. Why wasn't it him? He was older and had enjoyed a good life. He saw it more clearly now, realizing, like Crystal and for that matter, Sr., he had not let Candy go any more than they had let Jimmy go. It became clear to him that even now he carried Candy with him everywhere he went. She was always on his mind, even when he was out shopping, he would have conversations with her in his head. Not just her but a

NICE her. The her he never met because she was never as nice to him as his imagination made her out to be. Brad saw a little of himself in how Crystal responded to these sort of things in her life. Her tragedies are unique to her, his are unique to him and the other 7 billion people on Earth have troubles that are unique to them. Welcome to humankind. What's the one thing we have in common? We are all different. He liked her a lot and tried desperately to find the right words to convey his sympathy for her loss. He decided just to squeeze her hand gently while his hand was lying on hers. He made a commitment silently to himself that he wouldn't leave her unless she wanted him to leave. "Well, that just makes you human like me and the rest of us," He hoped that came out right, and tried to elaborate his personal situation as an example. "The pickles and jams where we sometimes find ourselves can really alter our direction in life. It did mine and whatever future I might have thought lay ahead has been irretrievably lost forever and from here forward, who knows?" he shook his head. "That's what happens. It seems most of us get derailed by our own bad luck or bad decisions even when we consciously try to make the best choices at the time. You just never know," Brad concluded. Crystal saw how hard he was trying to comfort her. She conceded that and smiled at him then she pulled her hand from under his for a second and rested it on top of his. Now she was comforting him. "I was able to get away and now I have a career," she managed a little smile at him. He asked her back, "Yes; and now look at me here with you. All that explains how you got here but how did I?" Crystal smiled, "Because you're a great guy." On the way past an attendant catches her eye and then looks at Brad and offers them a paper. "Anyone want a USA Today?" Crystal accepted the paper and laid it on her tray in front of her. She glanced down at the front-page story. A beautiful color photo that took up almost half the front page showed a group of young people, excited and having the time of their lives, along with a few adults on the field being cheered by the entire packed football stadium during yesterday's Baltimore Ravens game. A quick scan by Crystal revealed more details of the events surrounding the story of an amazing rescue of castaways that included two professional football players, Tony Mortensen of the Baltimore Ravens, Helen, his wife and their daughter Abby and his friend and college team-mate Maurice Munoz of the Miami Dolphins.

It told the story of a note in a bottle written and thrown out to sea by castaway, Abby Mortensen, 11 years old, and how it had been caught in a shrimp net by Levi Benjamin from Richmond Hill, GA. The story went on to describe how he and approximately 100 other computer enthusiasts used Google Earth to locate the castaways by zooming in as close as they could and scanning mapped out sections of the Atlantic Ocean along the southeastern seaboard. Then it described the excitement it caused when Eliza Martinez spotted an object on what appeared to her to be an uninhabited island. It was an amazing story with a happy ending. The U.S. Coast Guard gave all the credit to the young heroes stating that without their help it may have taken much longer or they may have never found the castaways.

Crystal pointed to the article and said to Brad, "This is a great story". Brad looked at the picture and said, "I don't think I would ever have thought of that." "Me either," Crystal agreed. The article went on to say, in recognition of the great American spirit of these fine folks, who were castaways, lost for nearly a year at sea and to recognize this incredible group of young people, all 100+ involved in the search to find them, the City of Baltimore, the Ravens NFL team and other kind individuals and businesses have invited this entire group of young people to the Ravens Stadium in Baltimore with free tickets for them and their families. The NFL is presenting individual awards of gratitude to be presented to Abby Mortensen, Levi Benjamin and Eliza Martinez by the NFL Commissioner, Rodger Goodell, and Baltimore Mayor Stephanie Rollins-Blake for their extraordinary efforts to locate the missing Mortensen family and Mr. Munoz. "That's an incredible story," Brad said.

Turning back to their conversation, Brad asked what drew her to his story. Crystal said this story seemed peculiar to her. She began, "I was alerted listening to my police band radio. I overheard enough of the story to find out the location of where the initial 911 call came from. They told me the dock where you left out of. Then I drove over there and talked to the Coast Guard Commander to get a few facts before going to the dock. He told me about your boat and where you and the squid were being taken. I next went to the dock where the boat was registered and talked to the dock owner who had called the Coast Guard hut. He gave me the name of the investigator assigned to collect background on the victims. I gave her a call and she told me about the argument at the restaurant. I called the hospital and they told me in the emergency room that you would probably be there a few more hours so I went to this little restaurant to see if there was anything there and to have some coffee and see what I could find out. I asked my waitress if she remembered you having breakfast there before you left on your trip and she was very eager to chat. She said several people there complained about, "that" couple. I asked her if she meant the couple that went missing, she said, yes; that the man was very upset about the girl's behavior the night before and they began to have a very big argument right here in the middle of the restaurant." Brad was a little embarrassed by that conversation but certainly didn't think of it as a big argument even though he was a little upset at the time. Crystal continued, "The waitress went on to describe how the two were trying to keep their voices down but everyone could hear them anyway. One waitress said it wouldn't surprise her if something bad had happened. I asked her what she meant? If she was saying the argument could have led to her being missing? She said, no, she was just saying it wouldn't surprise her," Crystal gave Brad a little grin. "Anyway," she continued, "the waitress finished her thought not wanting to speculate any further so I asked if anyone else overheard the conversation that I could speak to. I needed more information to finish she story, you know, to make it complete, beginning, middle and ending, a complete story worthy of being published, so I pursued deeper." Crystal went on, "There was another waitress here that was also there that morning and she totally agreed with the first waitress. So, I made some notes, and then went back to the Coast Guard Station and they told me the squid had been moved to the coroner's office in St. Petersburg, so that's where I went next and first saw the giant thing first hand. It was so disgusting and ugly and vile. The smell was sickening and I became nauseated when they cut it open...," she looked at Brad with sympathy in her eyes and said, "I'm so sorry this woman had to die this way." Brad was trying to look at Crystal as the face of Candy formed perfectly replacing Crystal's in his mind's eye. He stayed quiet as Crystal continued and he allowed the image of Candy's beautiful face to form so that he could look at her again. He wanted to hold on to her soft cheeks, look into her eyes and kiss her sweet face again but now his heart was broken. Tears started to form in his eyes but he blinked a couple of times and they were gone, he looked at Crystal again.

"It was incredible" Brad agreed, "I couldn't believe it either." He rubbed his watery eyes with his fingers and Crystal said she was sorry she came across so unsympathetic that morning but after throwing up, "I wasn't really at my best," she finished. "I understand, Crystal," Brad said. "I know you loved her Brad. I'm sorry this happened." "I know, Crystal," he said again. Then she said, "I could see that during my interview, it was in your face...and eyes. I could tell you were trying to make sense of it yourself. You were genuinely hurting. There were more things I wanted to learn, more questions I wanted answers to also. After learning all the details, what I wanted most was to apologize to you for my behavior but I didn't have the courage so I chose the follow up story angle." She couldn't contain a smile toward him as their eyes briefly met when she said those last few words. Brad blinked first and looked down as Crystal continued, "I began thinking about our interview and the things you said. You admitted to me you were afraid but I didn't see fear in you, I saw pain and anguish which is understandable from a man whose last recollection before waking here in this bed just a little while earlier, was of being unable to get into his boat. So, you tied yourself to the motor with part of the same rope that had a sea monster hooked on the end of it." "It was dead...I mean, when I did that, or close," Brad said. "Stop being so modest, Brad Reno."

Over the intercom, the captain indicated they were flying over the Grand Canyon and they had a good view out the left side. The man in the Hawaiian shirt leaned forward and blocked any line of vision Brad may have had out the window. Crystal was finishing up reading the article and never looked up. "Too bad we can't find a giant squid using Google Earth," Brad said under his breath. "That's about as close as I want to get to another one." Crystal didn't hear him.

CHAPTER 15

They landed in San Diego at 4 pm and made their way to baggage claim for Crystal to claim her two bags. Brad had his slung over his shoulder. A warm smell of diesel fumes was the first thing that hit Brad as he and Crystal walked out of the terminal. They got in line for a taxi. When they arrived at the Grand Colonial luxury hotel near the UC San Diego campus, Crystal noticed how helpful and attentive Brad was. She also noticed how nervous he was now. "Are you okay?" Brad looked at her and not wanting to appear to be staring, he turned his head quickly and said, "Yeah, I'm fine. How are you?" And he smiled back. "I'm fine, too. You just looked a little funny." "Yep, that's me alright," and he picked up her bags and carried them inside. Each gave their names at the desk and picked up the keys to their rooms. Brad turned toward Crystal, "Dinner?" he asked. "Sure," she answered. He turned toward the concierge, "Excuse me, sir?" he asked the uniformed man standing behind a podium near the front door.

"Can you recommend a place to eat around here?" "Yes, sir," the concierge spoke so deliberately. "Do you know what you would like to have? Seafood? Steaks?" Brad looked at Crystal and she tossed it back to him. "Doesn't matter to me," she said with a shrug. "Anywhere nice is fine." "Okay," the concierge started, "there are plenty of places nearby." He pulled out some literature of a few nice places. "Seasons 52 looks good, lobster ravioli," Brad read off the literature. "Oh, that sounds good," Crystal added. "Where is this place?" he asked the concierge. "Hold on," he said and picked up his phone, placed a quick call, spoke to someone quietly, then held the phone away from his ear and turned toward Brad. "I called them. They are usually booked but they will be able to reserve a table if you like." Brad looked at Crystal. "Sounds good to me," she said. "What time?" the concierge asked. Brad hesitated and looked at Crystal again. "In an hour?" she asked back. He looked at the concierge who went back to finish his call, then hung up. "Okay Mr. Reno, you have reservations in an hour at Seasons 52 and I hope you enjoy your meal. If you can come down about 15 minutes prior to your reservation, we'll get you a taxi and get you right over there." Brad looked at Crystal again. "Okay, dinner in an hour," she said. The elevator door opened and Brad moved so she could enter first as she did with a sweet, "Thank you." Brad entered and punched the second-floor button. "Which floor?" he asked. "Second, too," she said. He looked at her and she burst into a big smile,

"You look so nervous," she said smiling. Their rooms were next door to each other.

Forty-five minutes later, Crystal knocked on Brad's door. When he opened it, his mouth fell open. She looked incredible. Her blonde hair cascading beautifully, effortlessly around her shoulders, makeup and pink lipstick impeccable. Her dress was light and sleeveless with a pink floral print that ended several inches above her knees and she was wearing a beautiful wide braided gold necklace that lay just above the neckline of her dress and gold earrings that matched "Are you ready?" She asked. "Yeah, you look great," he managed to say and he could smell her perfume wafting in the corridor of the hallway. "I like your perfume," he said. "Thank you," she said as she smiled at him. She was enjoying this. She leaned close to him and sniffed his cheek. "You smell good too and you clean up very nice," she said with a big grin. He didn't think he was dressed up enough to be with her looking like that, though. He did shave and add a little after shave cologne of his own. He was wearing a print Golden Bear Golf shirt and slightly wrinkled tan khakis with Bass loafers. He didn't turn away this time and tripped over a wrinkle in the carpet but she deftly caught his arm to steady him. Embarrassed, he went on like it was nothing.

The taxi was right there at the door when they emerged from the lobby doors and were taken directly to the impressive Seasons 52 Restaurant less than a mile away in La Jolla. Brad's first impression of its motif was as a Mediterranean restaurant. It had a beautiful deck with decorative outdoor lighting for dining. They both thought that would be better than indoors on such a nice evening. The waiter brought menus and a wine list. The large plants behind them made a slight rustling sound occasionally as a slight warm breeze blew in from the ocean. The menu had seafood listed in abundance as well as lamb chops and pasta dishes. They hadn't eaten a real meal all day and decided they would try a few things.

Brad picked up the wine menu. "Wine?" he offered. "Of course," Crystal smiled again at him. He couldn't hold his grin in as he turned back to the menu. "How about a nice robust chardonnay from grapes grown right here in Napa Valley?" Brad playfully suggested. "It's highly recommended, I assure you, Ma'am," Brad finished with a western accent and a slight tip of his head. Crystal loved it. "Sounds perfect!" The service was very good. The waiter took their orders for an appetizer. A picture on the menu and description of a colorful salad and dressing, described as sesame-pistachio crunch on endive lettuce with fig balsamic dressing, sold that salad. They both asked for that. Crystal ordered the Caramelized Grilled Sea Scallops and Brad couldn't resist the California version of Southern-Style Shrimp and Grits just for comparison.

The talk went to the visit tomorrow at the research facility. They were both looking forward to going but Crystal's motive was to chase a story while his motive was different and he was anxious. Two waiters brought their meals and refilled their wine and water glasses and one asked if they needed anything. "No, thank you," Brad answered, "everything is perfect." He reached for his wine glass, lifted it to Crystal and she lifted hers, smiled and they both took a sip. The warm aroma of their seafood dishes circulating around their table made Brad's mouth water. He was hungry all of a sudden. Neither waited for the other to start, they both dug in and nothing but clinking and tapping and scrapping, plus a few other sounds that came from the table for a few minutes were, "ummm" and "This is delicious." and "Mine, too." "The wine was a good choice," "Thank you, would you like more?" "Sure!" Crystal gleefully conceded, and with a smile and another clink of the glasses, they had more wine together. "This is good," she indicated with her glass. "Good choice," she said again.

As they were finishing up their meal, Crystal picked up the almost empty bottle, poured the remaining teaspoon of wine into Brad's glass and said, "You finish it," took a deep breath and said, "I've had enough." That sentence brought Candy to Brad's mind for the first time today. They walked out to the lobby and the valet offered to get them a taxi. He followed them outside and they stood together under the lights in the perceptively noticeable warm air.

"I feel relaxed," she said and intertwined her arm around his and laid her head against his shoulder as they stood outside of the restaurant waiting for a taxi back to the hotel. Brad thought it felt good to have her there. It suddenly occurred to Brad, that he'd been in a funk for months. A light bulb just came on that he didn't even notice before was off. There had been a dark angry cloud over him that he hadn't been able to find the edge of. A heavy oppressive cloud that infused his mind with anger and had no end. Now that he has come to this realization, maybe he could start living life again. He paused thinking back. He had put himself in a self-imposed seclusion and started questioning everything. He knows now he was angry that he couldn't save Candy and he was also angry with the way their relationship was going. He loved Candy but he couldn't protect her, not in any form or fashion. That was a full-time job when it came to her. She gave him a clue that was the way it was going to be when they first started dating. He remembered plainly Candy asking him directly as seriously as she could in that playful sexy manner she had, she said "You think you can handle me?" She asked that very question. He should have said, "NO!" and walked away. From now on, he made a pledge to himself right then. If another woman ever asks him if he thinks he can handle her, he swore right then he will forever pick, NO! And to emphasize the point further, he added that succinct yet caustic Southern expression that goes, "not just no, but HELL NO!"

He remembered the last road trip he took with Candy. They had stopped at a vineyard, spent a little too much time wine tasting there and had several more glasses at an adjacent restaurant. When they got back on the road and going again Candy decided the wine was so good that she wanted more and was going to open a bottle that we had bought there and drink while he was driving. He didn't think she was serious but she was. She was just tipsy enough, or maybe he should be PC and say "buzzed" enough to be playful and rebellious. We had a corkscrew and she began to open the bottle. He told her not to do that, that he could get an open container ticket if we get stopped by the state patrol. Those guys don't play in SC or GA but, of course, she opened it and to be even more obstinate, she threw the cork out of the window and spilled some on herself in the process so then the whole inside of the car smelled like wine. What sound was it that he heard come out of his own mouth? The word that really fit is, "shrieked." He stopped the car right on the side of the interstate thinking he might be able to find that cork. Ha! This sounds so stupid now, thinking back on it. It was late afternoon, cars flying by, he didn't see it anywhere and it occurred to him how odd it must look to people driving by for him to be doing this. What if a cop stops and asks him what he's looking for? He couldn't say the cork to his wine bottle. So, he got back in the car, as stressed as an escaped convict on the run and hoping not to meet any police on the way, he stopped at the next exit with a hotel and checked in for the night.

Crystal distracted Brad's thoughts, "Brad, that was delicious, I'm stuffed. I could have filled up on that lobster bisque and roasted tomato flatbread with that wine." "Yes, I'm full, too. The wine was good. It's hard to find good California wines in South Carolina. If you happen to find one someplace, when you go back, you can never find that brand again," Brad added. "Oh yes, it was delicious," Crystal added sleepily.

The taxi pulled up and Brad opened the back door. Crystal got in and scooted to the middle but no further. Brad got in and found himself right up against her but she didn't move. He focused on getting them back to the hotel. It had been a long day and they were still on daylight savings time. They were both starting to feel the effects of the three-hour time change now. The clock on his phone said it was after one in the morning in Charleston. He gave the driver the name of the place and before Brad had finished his sentence, they were on their way.

Once back at the hotel, they walked through the lobby totally side by side, not looking in any direction but toward the elevator. One of guys at the front desk looked up and saw them, "Look at the zombies," he whispered to the lady beside him. She smiled at the two who looked like they were about to crash-land at any moment. The elevator door opened and Brad pushed the two. When they got to their rooms, Brad stopped and looked at Crystal. "I will see you in the morning." She looked at him, dreamy-eyed, reached up and put both arms around his neck and gave him a soft tender hug. "Okay" she said through the exhale of a big yawn..."I'll see you at 8:00 for coffee.....lots of coffee," she smiled at him a very sleepy seductive smile and said, "Goodnight," as she closed her door softly. He waited until he heard her deadbolt turn before he went to his room. He took one step and was at his own door. He looked toward Crystal's door, "Good night, Crystal."

The next morning at 8:00 Crystal knocked on his door and he was ready to go when he opened it. He thought she seemed a little embarrassed to see him. "Did I make it to the room before falling asleep last night?" She asked with a remorseful expression on her face. "You nearly did!" Brad joked back, "I only had to drag you the last ten or fifteen feet," he went on. "I'm sorry but I can't even remember the ride back," she laughed. "But I remember I had a wonderful time....up until we started back," She giggled and his heart melted. They had coffee with toast and jam for breakfast.

A blue Prius pulled up in front of the hotel at 9:00 and came to an abrupt stop beside Brad and Crystal, who were standing out front. "Good morning!" he said as he remotely lowered the passenger window to speak. "I'm Marshall England, are you Mr. Reno?" Brad nodded. Dr. England did a quick turn of his head and even quicker look around. "Looks like a nice place," he said. "Yeah, it's great," Brad answered. "I'm Brad, this is Crystal." "Nice to meet you. Hop in," Dr. England said, "and we'll get going. Traffic only gets worse around here."

He drove quickly through the neighborhoods he knew so well and started talking nonstop with a quick speech pattern louder and an octave higher than his normal voice because of the noises coming through his rolled down window. He talked fast and you had to listen close to catch it all. "You probably will be surprised at the interest in the subject matter you'll find here today given how rare you must believe these things are but they are quite common on the West coast and especially around here. So, after I informed my class that you were coming, it was them who wanted me to bring you up to LA so a few others could attend your talk as well," he said in one breath. "We have everything we need there to do our presentations and I think you will enjoy seeing the place. It's called, the Alta Sea facility, I think I sent you some info on it." "You did and it's impressive," answered Crystal. Dr. England went on. "Our budget has recently been increased due to the reasons I explained in my e-mail. The reduced fish population and so on. We can do more things now in partnership which stretches every dollar even more."

The Prius sped in and out of stop and floor-it traffic, but there were no major tie-ups this morning. They hopped on the Pacific Coast Highway and headed north to LA. Brad still thought it was one of the most scenic highways in America. Spectacular vistas of the Pacific Ocean and cliffs, the farms and fields all beautiful. They made good time after the traffic thinned out a little.

They exited the freeway and made it to the Port of Los Angeles. The Alta Sea port was very impressive as well. It had a look of recent modernization and immaculate care to detail. They passed a UC research ship moored against the dock. Dr. England swiftly found his usual parking spot and abruptly hit the brakes. They were given a quick overview by Dr. England on where things were as they were walking toward the dock. At the boarding plank a woman in her thirties came out to meet them. Dr. England started the conversation. "This is Dr. Ola Paget, communications director for Alta Sea and our liaison for the school," they all shook hands.

After a few introductions they boarded the research vessel before 9:30 am. Crystal had her handful of equipment including a hand-held microphone attached to an iPad and an additional laptop computer in a bag where everything was else stored. The ship was gray but it was unmistakably a UC ship. The university logo was all over it. And the first thing he noticed was the little yellow submarine on top. He wondered if it was the one from the news story. It too carried the UC logo. They were greeted by Dr. Bud Martin. Dr. England introduced everyone around and they began a tour of the ship Brad could tell they were so proud of. He would be too. They ended up in a conference room big enough for a medium-sized group to hold a meeting with audio-visual equip and a podium with the UC logo on front. It already had half a dozen folks including young graduate students and young professionals chatting among themselves when they walked in. Everyone was happy to meet Brad and Crystal.

Dr. England walked up to the podium and began to address the group in the small room, "Good morning ladies and gentlemen." The people here included expert professionals in their fields and students, all glad to be here. "I am extremely pleased to introduce to you to some very special guests this morning that have a unique firsthand knowledge in dealing with a colossal squid. A 32 foot long one to be exact." Everyone in the room knew there was only one man who has done that and a few smiled toward him. "We also invited Ms. Crystal Brook, from a St. Petersburg TV station, who did the story and who had the chance to see the giant animal up close during the autopsy, and most of you know of Mr. Brad Reno, who is the fisherman forced to confront this animal after it attacked his fishing boat killing his dear friend, Ms. Candace Cotton. We are all deeply sorry for your loss, Mr. Reno. We are extremely happy to have you both come speak to us today. Would you like to begin our meeting to get us off on the right track?" "Okay," Brad stood up and walked up to the podium as Dr. England sat in a chair close by. "Thank you, Dr. England."

He turned to the group. "Well, I am here to answer whatever questions I can about my encounter with the giant squid, I guess his name is Wuss now because I thought it was an octopus at first so I called it Wuss the puss, to belittle it in a way, I guess." He was a little nervous so he tried to say it like it was a little joke aimed at the giant squid. He thought that might get a smile from them but not this group, these were scientist, here to become educated on what he knew that might help them in their investigation and study of this animal. He looked toward Crystal and saw that she was smiling. It relieved him to know that words were coming out and his voice was heard, it was just a tough audience. He became serious, "My fiancé, Candy Cotton and I were on an overnight fishing trip about 20 miles out into the Gulf of Mexico off the coast of St. Petersburg, Florida. Sometime during the evening, she got up and walked out to the bow and was standing there holding the side of the windshield watching what we both thought was an unusual sight. Small and medium size fish were jumping in an unorganized fashion not as one might expect a school of fish to react, moving all together. It was dark but the moon was bright enough to see by." Several attendees started taking notes. "As quickly as Candy told me to look, I looked and appearing out of nowhere this massive appendage was coming over the side of the boat, it reached out about as far as it could and swept toward the bow exactly where Candy was standing. She had no chance, it swept her right overboard and all I could do was stand there and watch." Silence filled the room. Crystal was frozen as he filled in missing parts of the story. Brad continued, "I ran to see if I could see her but she was gone, along with the giant appendage and all the jumping fish," he paused and said almost too quietly to be heard, "everything became quiet in the water." He stopped to settle his thoughts and regain focus before continuing. "I stayed there that night hoping to find some sign of something from Candy. I decided the next day that I would stay there one more night before leaving. If it came back, I would try to kill it." Brad looked at the scientists for their reactions but there was no reaction from any of them. He went on, "I fashioned makeshift harpoons out of two oars and tied a line to one. I decided to wait it out.

It was late, completely dark out and I was sitting down when I heard fish began to jump. When one hit the boat, I got up and saw the tentacles breach the surface. The pattern of the creature seemed to indicate to me that he recognized the boat as the last place he found a meal and was coming back. When it attacked the boat, it swept in the same pattern as before. This time when it wasn't finding anything, it decided it would come in for a closer look. That's when I really got a good look at it. The pasty fleshy skin was disgusting enough but the tremendous eye I was sure had me pegged as suitable for eating. That's when I was able to get a clean shot at that eye and was hoping for the best. There was one other weapon in this monster's arsenal I had to avoid first. It could expel water through its siphon with such a powerful force, it would easily have knocked me off the boat if it had hit me directly," he went on. "After he was hooked on the makeshift harpoon line, he only seemed to be interested in getting away. He wasn't in such a hurry to eat me after that and I wasn't sure at the time but I believe he almost shimmered in the moonlight like he was changing colors in waves." "Chromatophores," interjected Dr. Martin, "They allow the squid to change colors as a way of communication or, when in pain or fearful," he added. "It definitely wanted to get away," Brad concluded.

Brad took a breather while Dr. Martin was readying a list of questions. "Mr. Reno, tell me if you have had any questions or insights after this encounter that have bothered you or maybe just made you curious?" Brad hesitated and began putting his thoughts in order because he had pondered this question since sitting on that boat. "My biggest question is," Brad took another breath and said what had indeed been bothering him for weeks. "Where did he come from? Or more precisely, where was Wuss born?" In Brad's mind he began thinking, there, it's out. I said it to the right people. Now I can go home. He continued talking out loud, "As far as insights go, I would say that these things do show signs of intelligence, but I want to be careful and not give him too much credit. He's not using crab leg crackers but he knew how to look for food and find it, something all carnivorous animals do and Wuss came back to where he had been successful at finding food before. Now think about this, he came to the surface, reached his tentacles out across the deck," Brad held his hand out like he was about to pick up a cup then used arm motion to illustrate the way the tentacle began to search potential food out by feel. "When his hubcap-sized eye came above the railing of the boat, I couldn't believe it. I thought he was going to climb on board." He paused again remembering the event and refocused his attention on telling his story. "Now I'm positive that monster was looking dead at me with that big ole eye. I couldn't ever have imagined that a sea monster with an eye big enough to see Uranus from here was looking right at me less than ten feet away and he wanted to catch me just for the sole purpose of having me for dinner like the Jack and the Beanstalk giant," he paused. "Except with Wuss, there was no anger, remorse or malice, just hunger. I don't know if hunger was its only motive. I don't know anything really," Brad stopped there. The scientists had all the other facts about Wuss. They had seen the pictures and the autopsy report. It was the only resource of its kind to exist, but Brad had them all captivated, even Crystal. Getting back to the point he wanted to make, he closed with this. "I want to make it clear. It occurred to me that I may have gone overboard with my appraisal of his intelligence at first because I witnessed his tenacity in the one skill he had that I did see...and that was in finding and capturing food. Wuss was searching for food the way he was genetically programmed to, not out of anger, fear or in defense of its babies. That's the good news, the bad news, Wuss was carnivorous and here he was in an area where boats go by all the time. If there are any more of these things around here, and there are," he paused, "well, we already have seen evidence that they can pluck people off boats and docks when they get hungry enough. It's like getting payback from the fish that have avoided being caught and have brought in a hero to fight back against the fishermen. Nothing this size to our knowledge has ever been spotted here before, so my question is, how did he get here? Did the smaller fish pay him?" A few of the folks laughed at that. "I'm kidding but I believe the question is relevant and one I hope we can find time to discuss." All the room was listening and all the scientific minds were attuned to hear that one phrase or observation that might lead them in a new direction toward more new information and maybe eventually a breakthrough. As he was about to look toward Dr. England for permission to end his talk right here, a young man who turned out to be a student in the Marine Biology program raised his hand. "Yes?" Brad asked. "So, you believe the aggressive nature of Wuss may have been no more than random searching for food?"

"Yes, that's my opinion but I don't know. This one this time maybe," he started again, "What we know about Wuss was that he was starving. He had outgrown his surrounding food supply. I watched the giant tentacle as it was exploring the boat methodically looking for its next meal, taking its time. It didn't look as healthy as some do in pictures I've seen since then. It came up to the boat and performed the same maneuver, almost identical to the maneuver it made when it swept Candy overboard. This move caught my attention and I recognized it right away. I was able to calm down and move around the boat after that until its eye breached the railing. That's when it gave me the first evidence that it had some level of intelligence. When an animal's eyes can lock on mine, I recognize that as intelligence to some extent. That's one reason I think we talk to animals. It did obviously have a mission, to find food. Other than that, the other thing was that," he paused, "I assumed that it was nocturnal. I sat there in the boat all day not once fearful that it would attack until it got dark. I started thinking about the behavior I was observing. In my mind, I was trying to cut it down to size....my size...something I could handle, therefore, I decided to back off a little and think about what I had witnessed. Comparing it to other animals, the anteater came to mind and how it searches for food using its tongue in a similar fashion to randomly reach down into convoluted ant hills to capture food before laying eyes on it. So, I decided, this monster is not a killer with any animus as its motive, it's just a starving carnivorous opportunistic wild animal searching for food in an area that's been cleaned out. No different than a lion, alligator or anteater." He turned to leave the podium.

"Thank you for your insight, Mr. Reno," then a hand went up. He stopped and thoughtfully turned around. "Yes," Brad recognizes the young lady, "Mr. Reno, do you know how Wuss got to Florida?" "Open borders?" he said back in a joking way. No one laughed again. "I was trying to figure that out. A fisherman friend told me they ride the currents. Figure out which current he rode in on and trace it backwards like hurricane storm trackers and see if we can figure it out. We'll know when we find it because there will be a lot of giant squids around there." Brad didn't want to sound like a paranoid weekend fisherman to these scientists, but thought this may be his best opportunity to get this out. "I have no scientific proof of this. It is just a theory but if what I suspect is true, there could be thousands like Wuss and I believe there may be a way to prove it. I've been trying for the life of me to figure out where Wuss came from and how he got where he was. There are several possibilities." Brad started unloading his thoughts. "If Wuss was born in the Southern Atlantic

Ocean, he could have veered off course while riding the jet stream current or he might have come from the North Atlantic. They certainly grow the crabs bigger up there and whale are seen migrating through there. There is another possibility that the mother gave birth near the cape of South America or the South Pacific but that is a very long way from where Wuss wound up." All the scientists were intrigued by Brad's theory up until now. "So, where did Wuss come from?" Brad paused to give them a moment to ponder the thought before he dropped the bombshell. "Better yet, another way to ask the same question is where was he and his hundreds of siblings born? Many may not have survived or may have been carried far off like Wuss, but I believe the majority remain in a radius of wherever they were born. Anyway, wherever he is from is where we will find more.... many more, and if they all get as big as Wuss, well, I don't think it'll be too difficult to spot them and I for one would like to know so I could mark that off my bucket list of places I'd like to visit." Several agreed that there was reason enough to look into the possibility that if there is an increase of attacks in a certain area it may well be a public health menace like sharks spotted off the shore, "Yes, everybody out of the water!" Brad concluded.

"Well, Mr. Reno, to bring you quickly forward to what we believe we have discovered thus far is that there is evidence of a rather large population of a relative to this monster in the Sea of Cortez. We aren't sure if any are as large as Wuss. The variety found here off the Baja peninsula are the Humboldt squids and they average usually less than seven feet in length," he paused as he was deciding in his own mind why a seven-foot-long squid shouldn't be considered a giant. "They populate this area all year round by evidence of eyewitness sightings and those caught in nets. We believe they are thriving in our vast oceans primarily because they stay near the bottom and mostly just pass by an area and come to the surface only when hunger drives them upward to search for food. So, they hunt as they ride currents vast distances. The only thing out there above them on the food chain is the sperm whale so a researcher may try to locate and follow a pod of whales in order to locate a colossal squid. That's how the first live giant was captured on film."

To get a better picture of where they were talking about, Crystal pulled up a picture of the Baja peninsula on her laptop. The scientists all gathered around Brad to help if they could to identify any areas in the radius of this area and see if there had been any other recorded attacks of any kind to fishermen, divers or sports enthusiasts. The scientists started talking to each other and pointing to locations near the Baja Peninsula, Southern California area. Brad turned away from the computer as Crystal took hold of the mouse and zoomed back from the picture. It now included Central America. She had a thought as she judged distances in her mind. "Brad?" she asked. "Yes, Crystal," he answered. "Brad, what about the Panama Canal?" "What?" he queried. "Do you think Wuss could have come through the

Panama Canal?" she clarified. He looked closer at the map and it was the shortest distance from the West Coast so Brad was looking closer. "That's a possibility," stated Dr. Martin. "There is evidence they are on the West Coast. The shortest distance from there to the Gulf of Mexico is through the Panama Canal." They decided that this was worth looking into. Ideas started coming from the others. "We can see if the employees along the canal have spotted any," said one student. "We can start putting tracking devices on some around here and see where they go." "All good ideas," Dr. England spoke out loud.

Brad thanked everyone for inviting him and said that he hoped he had been helpful. Crystal motioned him to have a seat near her. Dr. England walked back up to the podium and from there spoke to Brad and Crystal directly. "We value the time you spent leaving everything behind for these few days away from your work. Tomorrow, Dr. Martin and I plan to take the UC 'Think Tank' out, which is what we call our submersible, to take some photos of an area we have been studying in the California Gulf also known as The Sea of Cortez. Our submersible is only two-manned but you could each go separately with me or Dr. Martin, each trip last little more than an hour. We are observing and taking pictures of the species of fish and flora in a designated area so Ms. Brook?" As he addressed her, "If you would like to, you may ride with Dr. Martin and Mr. Reno can ride with me later. Are you up to it?" he directed the nod toward Crystal, she nodded back excitedly without hesitation. Her excitement was hard to miss, her smile is so beautiful and she was smiling big now. Brad looked away and started thinking about it. He wasn't quite as enthusiastic as Crystal but he stayed with her in the front row and listened to Dr. Martin discuss the mission for the next morning. Now that they have additional crew, there needed to be a few changes. He introduced the next speaker and sat next to Crystal and Brad.

The student introduced himself as Cris Prince, from San Diego. He was in his third-year invertebrates studies and was curious about these squids. There are very few resources to be found about them because there is very little solid evidence of them. He said, "I have found a couple of cases that are easy to look up that include more evidence now of their existence and how the sightings are becoming more frequent. Here is one." He pulled up a picture of one Brad had missed. Cris went on, "This colossal squid was found in the waters near Tasmania caught in a fishing net. Autopsy of the giant found its stomach contained the tips of other squid's tentacles and several beaks, providing further proof they are indeed cannibalistic. The colossal squid is equipped with two tentacles, eight arms and is the largest of all the giant squids exceeding 60 feet from tip to tip. It has circular hooks embedded in its tentacles and is the only giant squid to have these besides the Humboldt squids who are native to these waters and the California gulf." He then pulled up the most recent video of a giant squid taken only months ago, spotted briefly by a team of investigators, between 2000 to 3000 feet deep nearly adjacent to where Wuss was encountered, directly South of Louisiana. He then went back in history of a similar photo and story he had found. It included one of the first photos of this colossal squid species and was estimated to be 24 feet long. The photo was captured by researcher, Tsunemi Kubodera in 2006 from the waters south of Tokyo. Brad was listening but Crystal had her video camera on and was still taking notes.

That evening they were dropped off at the hotel where they were staying. Brad couldn't help noticing how beautifully decorated and softly lit the hotel lobby was. He could hear soft music from a lounge with a piano bar down the hallway.

They met for dinner an hour later and walked to a seafood restaurant nearby recommended by the concierge. The lights were low with candles on the tables. They were seated in a quiet area at a table set for two with a white linen tablecloth. The waitress came by with menus, poured water into their water glasses and asked if they wanted to order drinks. "What would you like to drink?" Brad asked. "A glass of wine would be good," Crystal suggested. "A bottle would be better," Brad added. "Yes, it would, thank you." Brad smiled and she smiled back. "Is Pinot Grigio, okay?" he asked her as he stared at the wine list and read about one that sounded like it would be good. "Sure," she answered. He picked a mid-range highly rated California brand.

"We'll try this one," he told the waiter. "Very good, Sir. I'll go put in your drink order," and left.

Brad looked around at the small crowd, a few folks at the bar, glasses bumped together as a waiter was clearing the table next to them faster than a speeding bullet. "So, what did you think of the place today?" Brad asked. Crystal began, "I thought it was incredible. I didn't know they had such a nice ship." "Me neither," Brad agreed. "How do you feel about going out with them tomorrow?" "Excited!" She exclaimed. "I thought we were just going to the educational portion of the place. I didn't know they had an expedition scheduled for tomorrow. It was great for them to invite us along. I have my video camera and my protector, so I'm good," He tilted his head up toward her from his menu. She liked it when she could make him turn his head and look at her like that. She thought he was handsome.

The waiter brought the chilled bottle of wine to the table, presented it to him first, then to Crystal, opened it and poured a small amount in his glass, he picked up the glass, sniffed the fragrance as he swirled the golden liquid gently then lifted the glass to his lips and took a small sip. "Good," he said. He turned to Crystal, "Would you like him pour you a sample to taste?" he asked. "I trust you," she said. The waiter poured the wine for them and asked each their choices for dinner.

Bonito prepared to order, was the Fresh Catch of the Day, highlighted on a small blackboard they saw when they came in, they both decided to order that. Their waiter assured them it was the most requested item of the evening. He gave his final approval to all their choices and headed back to the kitchen. Crystal took her glass before she sat it down and raised it toward Brad. "Brad, I want to thank you for coming with me. You don't know what it means to me." "I'm glad I came too," he said. "Thank you for inviting me." They talked a little about where they grew up and where they went to school. Brad informed her that he went to Business School after he served in the Navy. He travelled for over twenty years as a pharmaceutical rep and retired after his divorce. He wanted to be more available if his daughter needed him so he settled in here close to the ocean.

When their meals arrived, the fragrance of the baked white fish alone made his mouth start watering, especially as he squeezed a lemon wedge over the tender flaky fish on top of rice pilaf with a few capers scattered about. A side salad with a vinaigrette house dressing, salt and a pepper mill were all Brad needed to make it perfect. "Smells delicious!" Crystal said. "Yeah, very fresh, tastes like it's right off the boat," Brad replied. They enjoyed their meal and Brad turned the now empty bottle of wine upside down and set it carefully back in the chiller. "Another dead soldier," he said referring to the wine bottle. "He was a good man," Crystal concluded and saluted. After dinner, the weather was so nice, they veered off the path on the walk back to the hotel and decided to go for a walk on a short boardwalk and nearby dock. The breeze was warm off the water and the moonlight shone high in the sky. The song, Moonlight Feels Right, popped into his head. Brad thought about reaching to hold her hand. He had to remember that this wasn't a date and he didn't want to overstep his boundaries especially still holding on to memories of Candy like he was. She kept walking close beside him though, bumping against him with every step, not seeming to notice that it wasn't a date. Brad wasn't sure anymore either. "I'm glad you came with me," Crystal said, looking out across the beach to the Pacific Ocean. The breakers created a calming rhythmic rush that comforted and set a mood. "You said that already," Brad answered, "Me too," he said again. "I did?" She said with a high giggle. "Must be the wine," she smiled. "Yes, the wine was great," he added smiling back. They stood out there making small talk a few minutes longer before calling it an evening. They made it back to the hotel and to the two rooms they occupied that were next door to each other, 210 and 212.

They would be picked up the next morning at 8:00 and taken to the airport where they will leave out by helicopter and meet up with the research ship off the coast in an area normally reserved for fishing. They will be taking pictures and video to study to try to find answers to why the fish population had decreased. They made arrangements to meet at 7:00 for breakfast then to the airport for the helicopter ride. They swapped hugs and sweet cheek kisses and to Crystal, that made Brad the perfect gentleman. When they said goodnight at her door, Brad wanted to kiss her beautiful lips but held back. She thought he was going too but he stopped short again. They would see each other at breakfast, 7:00.

The next morning Brad and Crystal were sitting at a table having coffee and croissants with butter and jam when Dr. England came into the dining room. He saw them and walked to their table. "Good morning," he said. "Hey Marshall, have a seat?" Brad offered. "I believe I will, Oh, those look good" he said, pointing to the croissants. He sat down and ordered coffee.

"Here's an update. Dr. Martin and his team and crew moved the ship with the, "Think Tank" back from the Port of Los Angeles last evening and is right now headed toward an area west of the Sea of Cortez. We will take a helicopter and meet him there...see what they found." He picked up a warm croissant and began to butter it. "He and his team plan to take the ship with the "Think Tank" out early today to start their observations. They should be getting back in shortly after we arrive, then you," he looked at Crystal "and Dr. Martin are taking a sister ship RS-1 out while the RS-2 sub is checked over. We will take RS-2 later," he said, as he looked at Brad and started putting Knott's Berry Farm strawberry jam on his croissant. He looked again toward Crystal as he was quickly chewing a big bite and swallowing a mouthful of coffee. After a quick gulp he continued talking. "You should be able to get some good video if you want to as well." "Oh, I'm ready," she said. "I've got everything I need right here," and tapped her computer bag.

After his quick cup of coffee and cellphone call to

the small airport nearby, they packed into the Prius. Traffic was heavy but they got there straight away. Brad saw Crystal snap a photo of a blimp sitting on the tarmac. They followed Dr. England to their helicopter, met the pilot and strapped themselves in. The pilot wasted no time in getting off the ground as soon as the control tower said he was clear to go. The populated areas began thinning out as they headed toward Baja California.

Brad was transfixed on the view of the terrain from this vantage point on the helicopter. He had never been to this part of the country. The desolate sunbaked landscape wasn't completely deserted but nearly. White sandy roads led to the white sand beaches of the Sea of Cortez. Flying over, you could see Ensenada Baja, California. It was big and busy but the traffic was slow or stopped. What caught his attention were the colors that looked so out of place out here. The different brilliant hues of the blue waters and the separate emerald greens to blended shades of aquamarines, all these colors shone brightly and sparkled brilliantly in the bright sunshine against the barren white sandy roads and the many contrasting colors of the landscape. The sun bleached out some of those colors. The closer he looked at the hills, he could make out brilliant oranges, golds, even reds the color of Georgia red clay. He could see some hills with different colors of layers of rock with complete separation of the colors. Someone described a place like this as, "painted hills" he thought that describes this place too. He could also see outlines of coral reefs and oyster beds in the clear waters along small islands jutting up from reefs that have come close to the surface. Some of the higher rocky hills that outline the jagged borders of the sea looked yellow and brown and sparse of vegetation. Huge rocks with sharp edges and lines of erosion from centuries of the Sun's radiant heat in the summers and freezing winters, was a warning to others planning to venture into the higher elevations, that it only gets harder from here. Everything is dead now except cacti of all shapes and sizes.

With no water, there is nothing but the brown straw of long dead vegetation. The contrast of dead terrain against the backdrop of a vibrant blue full-of-life ocean seemed oddly normal here at the Sea of Cortez. As they headed out over the pristine waters, Dr. England turned to Brad, "The ship is right up here!" Brad and Crystal both looked where he was pointing. They could see the ship below as they started descending.

Brad thought the ship looked mighty small to be landing on with a helicopter but they did it anyway. He took in the panoramic view of contrasting mediums for the last time before exiting the helicopter with the others and catching up to them on the UC ship. As he was walking along close to the edge, A "Swoosh!" and solid form flew out of the water right beside where he was standing. His heart nearly stopped. "What was that?" he blurted out. Dr. England looked out over the railing. He could see several Mobula rays performing acrobatic flips out only yards from the ship. Dr. England said "These are rays, like Manta rays but these are called

Mobula rays. This is part of their mating ritual.....belly flops!" he kept walking. Crystal looked at him and mouthed the question with a sly grin, "You okay?" Brad nodded back. It reminded him of something more ominous, a sign that a monster may be lurking below on his way to the surface to devour the smaller fish there. He didn't say anything because he realized that these rays jumping may not be an unusual sight here and he didn't want to look like a pathetic victim suffering from post-traumatic stress syndrome. He kept silent but kept scanning the ocean.

Ola from the Alta Sea facility came along to take some readings of her own for a separate study and approached the landing party as the helicopter took off. That's when Brad saw a yellow sub in the water on the other side of the ship and sitting low in water. "Is that the one we are taking out?" He asked Dr. England. "Yes, we will be taking this one out next while the crew gives Dr. Martin's a good systems check." Ola added, "Dr. Martin is still down. He should be up within the next hour. Come in and we'll bring you up to date on what he's doing." She turned and everyone followed her toward the radio room. Dr. England went on to answer Brad's question. "Yeah, we can only move one per ship for now. We brought this one up with Ola's crew. They will be looking at the reefs not far from here for any population changes. Dr. Martin will be back soon. Is everything going according to plan?" Dr. England asked Ola. "Yes, everything is on schedule," she said.

When they were within just a few steps of the radio

room hatch, the radioman stepped out of his seclusion to meet them and began waving and calling for them to hurry over. He was holding his headset in his hand with the wire stretched over his shoulder and began reporting as emphatically serious as he could, trying but failing not to panic. He called them all to listen, everyone froze, "The RS-2 is sending a distress call!" he relayed, "Listen!" A disturbing call could be heard from the radio originating from the research sub. They were urgently reporting that they had lost control of the small sub. Dr. England, Brad, Crystal and Ola, the Alta Sea liaison, rushed in, in time to hear the distress call over the speaker. "Looks like the squids down here are taking a liking to us," came the crackling report over the speakers from Dr. Martin in RS-2. "We can see several swimming around at least four have attached themselves to the sub. I repeat multiple squids, 4 to 7 ft. in length, are attaching themselves to the outside of the sub and now have added so much weight that they are dragging us down. We no longer have control and are asking for help. Do you have any ideas? Come back?" The five of them, Brad, Crystal, Dr. England and Ola the Alta Sea employee, and Jack the radio operator all looked at each other at once. Their initial shock registered just long enough to be replaced by the first idea to emerge. These were professionals who understood they had to find a way right now to help the sub. The first to speak was Brad. "Where are they?" he asked. Jack answered, "They were no more than 150 yards from here on their way back when Dr. Martin reported the first one had latched on and a whole squad started circling them." Dr. England then stated directly, "Well, the only thing I can think to do is to go get them. We have to send the other sub down there and bring them back." Brad looked at Dr. England, "Is that possible?" He asked. They all understood the urgency and the danger of doing that. They even brought up the real danger that it could meet the same welcoming party and then there would be two subs that needed saving. Dr. England said, "If we can get a tow line on it, we can haul it in." "How are we going to do that? Has it ever been done before?" Brad asked. Ola answered. "We can attach a cable to the top of the sub. If it is upright, you should be able to find it and hook up to it. That's not the problem. The problem is, it will have to be attached manually. A diver has to swim along outside because there is no watertight chamber to allow exiting this submersible underwater and with the squids in the way, a remote-control arm isn't likely to work. So, a diver will have to pull the cable from our sub, swim over, remove any squids in the way and attach it to the other. Jack, are there any divers on board?" "No, but it won't take long to get one," he said. "I can have one here in an hour, maybe less." Dr. England pondered that. "That may be too long," he said, "they probably are getting low on air now." Then a quiet voice spoke out. "I'm a diver," Brad said quietly, "so I guess that's me." He gave a half-hearted smile as he glanced around hoping someone else had a better idea. No one did so no one questioned the two men volunteering. There wasn't enough time to discuss it further. The people who knew them were not surprised and Crystal knew before anyone else. She started videoing the beginning of this plan to rescue RS-2 as it went into action. Jack called the Coast Guard and explained the emergency. They dispatched two Coast Guard vessels with dive teams immediately to their location. Jack, then got on the ship's intercom, sounded the alarm and began to relay orders to the crew that they had an emergency and the other sub needed to be checked and readied for departure immediately. The crew launched into action and worked quickly together to check the sub for operation and communication systems.

Dr. England was giving Brad his last-minute instructions as he was getting into a wetsuit.

"We carry the line down to the sub, attach it and haul it in before they run out of air. That's the plan." Dr. England took command of the rescue and succinctly described his hastily thought-out plan. Straight forward and time was wasting. Crystal jumped in, "What about the squids?" Crystal thought she knew what was coming next. Brad spoke up, "If I can get close enough to attach a line, you bet a few squids aren't going to stop me. I'll try to a knock 'em off, hook it and get away quick then you can hoist it up." Dr. England nodded and turned his attention in prepping his sub.

Brad looked at Crystal. She knew he didn't want to go but she knew she couldn't stop him either. He would go anyway. Then Crystal did something she had never done before, she looked directly into Brad's eyes, closed the gap in a second and kissed him hard on the lips, gave him a strong hug then pulled back. "I'll see you when you get back." She said and forced a difficult smile. Brad had a way of saying the right thing at difficult times. It could reduce her anxiety instantly. Again, he did not disappoint. "How do I look?" he looked up at her with his full scuba outfit on. "Like half of a Barbie and Ken Frogman Set," she said. He "huffed," giving a sort of acknowledgement and said, "Sure you don't want to go?" He asked with a smile she couldn't help returning. They just stood there a second longer looking into each other's eyes. Crystal smiled bigger, gave him another quick kiss and said, "Good luck." Marshall was in the sub.

Jack volunteered to ride shotgun with Dr. England to keep communications established, but Dr. England knew it was vitally important he stay here and do everything he could to keep communications open and that he would leave his radio mic open. They both knew if they lost contact with the sub before they could get a line on it, they may never find it again. In Brad's mind it was a no-brainer and even more important, time was being wasted. Crystal saw her opportunity, "Let me record this from inside the sub," she stated flatly. "I don't know Ms. Brook. This is way more than we expected." She looked at Brad who smiled at her and looked back at Dr. England. "That's what we're here for, to be of assistance." She ran to get her bag, grabbed it and climbed into the sub. She looked back at Brad, "Let's go!" she yelled.

Brad checked his regulator and jumped into the water, found handholds on the sub and stuck an upward pointing thumb in front of a forward-facing porthole. He saw Crystal smiling back. He felt the propellers aerating the water and the sub began moving forward and downward.

Dr. England began looking on his radar scope for a signal from its sister sub. The water became darker as they went deeper. He didn't want to waste time but with Brad holding on to the outside, he didn't want to lose him and it caused a big shift in controlling the steering with the additional weight on the hull. Jack indicated to Dr. England over the radio that the other sub was sending out the emergency beacon. The signal came from below them somewhere around 100 feet, a dangerous depth for any diver, much less for someone who had never attempted such a daring rescue but they all knew time was something they just didn't have a lot of. They had to put a cable on that sub quickly before they lost communication with it for what could be forever.

CHAPTER 16

The call had gone out to the Coast Guard and they were on their way. The USCG also had a submersible and was planning to use it, unfortunately, they were at least an hour away which would be too late to help the men inside the sub. Any moment they could lose the signal and with the loss of signal would be a death sentence for the crew if they were unable to return to the surface. Oxygen would be gone long before they would have time to be rescued alive. No time to contemplate what ifs or think about what could go wrong, just go, in and out. Brad peaked around to the front of the porthole to look in. He motioned with a nod and thumbs up that he was ready. Marshall got in front of the porthole to sign language Brad. He first gave the okay sign with his thumb and forefinger making the sign. Brad signed back. Then he mouthed the words, "The sub is going down," Brad nodded that he understood and Marshall pointed straight down and Brad indicated he was following so far. Then Marshall closed and opened his hands again. Brad nodded and held up two fingers to show he was getting it. Two hands are ten feet, two are twenty. The hands opened and closed eight more times and Brad was nervous now because he knew he would not have much time at all. Jack must have been working on his time table at that depth. He tapped on the porthole and caught Brad's attention. Marshall pointed to his watch and indicated 10 minutes to get down there find and attach the cable and have time to get back. Marshall made sure Brad had plenty of time for his ascent, if he needed it, so as not to get the bends from the nitrogen bubbles that can form in a diver's bloodstream and can cause severe cramping, debilitating pain and death from an air embolism simply from ascending too quickly.

Brad gave the thumbs up back to the two watching from a porthole. "Here we go!" Marshall signaled back with his own thumbs up signal. Brad continued to hold tight to the sub handholds and stay visible in front of the porthole so someone could keep an eye on him. Dr. England followed the headings emanating from a signal below. This kind of descent for Brad would have normally been something he would not do in a million years. Now he realized, that's not even the worst part. He was going into a bunch of squids, and some may be bigger than him, to knock them off the outside of the sub with just the wrench he stuck under his weight belt as he was leaving the ship. He would have to figure it out when he got there, he had no other choice. He looked at his depth gauge and now they were approaching fifty feet. He started feeling the pressure closing in after 30 feet. He swallowed and felt his ears pop adjusting to the pressures. He looked ahead and saw a few medium and small colorful fish catching and reflecting light from the surface. He watched a school of smaller fish dart together and that's when he saw his first squid. It darted toward the yellow sub below him about twenty feet. Then he saw two more. They were big, but suddenly a shadow moved beneath him that at first, he mistook for the bottom. It was big but Brad was unable to lay eyes on anything large enough to make that shadow. Another squid came up and attached itself to their sub. Brad shimmied his way down to where he could reach it and smashed a tentacle with his wrench, causing it to drop off while others were in sight zipping in and away. A cloud of ink with an ascending trail was left by the one he had smacked as it sped away with the speed of a giant bullfrog.

He looked ahead and could see the top of the stranded sub. It had at least 6 or 7 squids just hanging on it. He tapped the sub he was hanging on to indicate to Dr. England and Crystal that he saw the sub. They both nodded that they understood. Crystal was taking a video of as much as she could see from her limited vision through the ten-inch porthole. Brad had the rescue cable from his sub in his hand and carried it allowing it to freely unwound from its reel as he swam toward the trapped sub. Crystal could see him swimming away from her toward the other sub, his fins waving slowly and rhythmically and seemingly without a care in the world dragging the cable along. "Be careful," she whispered to herself. No sooner did he reach it than he felt a punch in his back. Crystal saw the attack, "Oh my God, Brad!" She gasped at the same time he gasped and he turned his head to see half a dozen squids zipping past. He returned to his job and used the wrench to try to beat the squids away from the stranded sub. One wrapped a tentacle around his arm and he felt a sharp stabbing pain. He used the wrench to smash its mantle and push it away. Many started darting in to make a meal of the injured squid as is part of their cannibalistic nature. He returned to his work and used the wrench to connect the cable to the other sub. Once complete, he tapped on the trapped sub and looked into the porthole. Dr. Martin and another passenger waved with the biggest grin he ever saw on another man. Smiles and thumbs up from inside at least meant they were still okay for now. Dr. Martin got on the radio inside the sub and was able to talk directly to Dr. England. The familiar voice was staticky but came through good enough. "Hello RS-2 how's it going, Bud?" The deadpan humor of Dr. Martin wasn't lost on Crystal, though she didn't know him very well. She started cataloging his actions. He's good under stress. She could tell that right away. "Oh, fine Marshall, we were just enjoying the scenery." Dr. England responded, "Yes, you guys have really lost track of time now. It's getting late."

Brad knew he had to return to the surface slowly. He was over 90 feet deep and he surmised that it was about time to leave and so did RS-1 with RS-2 in tow. He glanced at his regulator to confirm that as he kept lookout for other squids, they were quick and aggressive and he didn't trust them not to hit him in the back at any second. The rescuers began their ascent, every once in a few seconds a squid would scoot past leaving an inky contrail. One brushed up against Brad and a second hit him hard in the right kidney. He lost hold of the rope and was pushed away from it. He took a swipe at his silent attacker as it came back and managed to block the next pass. It left an ink blotch and scooted away. Brad lost sight of the rope and didn't see the sub anymore so he slowly continued ascending, watching carefully in all directions.

Once on the surface Crystal saw that Brad wasn't there. "Where's Brad," she called. "Where is he? We have to go back." "Hello!" came a yell from the water. Brad was about forty feet away and swimming back. He was barely out of the water when Crystal ran over and hugged his neck. "You were wonderful." she told him. He smiled a little at her, nodded his head, leaned in and offered his cheek up for her kiss. She wrapped her arms around his neck again and kissed his smiling cheek. Getting out of RS-2, Doctor Martin, who has a great sense of humor, got on his knees and kissed the deck. He looked like he was the happiest man alive. He tried to describe how it felt to be in that sub as a whole squad of squids attacked them. To show he still had a sense of humor, he said, "I think those squids either like me, or don't like me but I can't decide which. This is the second time I've been roughed up by these ding dongs. It ain't fun getting smacked around. You know how it feels when you're in a giant hollow bowling ball underwater and you're being rammed by squids that are bigger than you are? That's how this feels, just like that." "Or a soccer ball?" asked his boat-mate. "Yes, soccer," he hesitated. "Well, not exactly soccer because that's just kicked around. I think it felt more like underwater rugby and we were the rugby ball." The crew laughed.

Dr. Martin began to relay the story of how they got into this fix. "We were talking to each other and finishing up recording out the portholes. I was at the controls, hands on the rudder controls while Dr. Rivera operated the cameras. The activity started picking up and at first they just bumped up against us, then a couple latched on, that's when we lost control." Bud then began to get animated, moving all around the room bumping into things. "It was incredible, simple as that! Did I tell you this was the second time this happened to me? I think these things like me!" he went on, "We were upside down at times and every other way. You could feel the boat being knocked around and jostled," he said, "hit over and over, tossed and then hit more, then slammed, rammed and jammed. We were turned upside down then down side up and more than once and finally we were held tightly like a football running back would hold a football, tucked in as we started falling into that abyss and you could feel scraping against the hull of the ship. It felt like parts of the sub were being broken off and what was left was being twisted and deformed. We tried to call as soon as they stopped bouncing us around enough to get our balance. We finally stopped long enough to get on the radio and managed to get contact. We didn't know what was next in store for us and all we could do was wait." Then he took a well-deserved breath.

Doctor Martin was exhibiting an elevated boost of adrenaline and couldn't stop talking, plus his sense of humor was spot on. If he couldn't keep your full attention while he was telling his story, he would get up and start acting out the parts and he was hysterical at times. Now, he was showing the faces he and Dr. Rivera were making as they were flipping around. He stopped laughing for a second to think about it. It was starting to sink in that it was more like having a near death experience. He started shaking, realizing that he was within a smidgen of being lost and dying on the bottom of the sea in a small submersible. Ola handed him a soft drink. "Thanks," he said, and sat down.

Crystal had been making notes and recording the unofficial debriefing as well as the entire event from the sub. She had it all and was finishing up when Brad came up to her, "Hey," she looked his way; then she reached out her hand to him and smiled. "are you okay?" he asked her. She grinned big, "I'm fine," she said, "and you were great." The crew had raised the RS-1 out of the water for a systems check. Ola and another crew member were checking the operation of RS-2. Everything checked out but there was damage on the exterior that needed to be scrutinized further. She wanted to take the RS-2 to a nearby dock in Ensenada for a better look. It was no more than a thirty-minute ride in the sub along the surface, so Ola and another crew member boarded RS-2 and headed in that direction, then Dr. England approached them both. "Well, we are here to do some work so we're going to move to our next site. Maybe you can get a better impression of what is around here and round out your story if you're up for it." Everyone had calmed down except for Dr. Martin. They could still hear him two doors down. Crystal said, "He is a hoot?" "Yes, he is our therapy and we are his," Marshall smiled a little, then he went on to explain. "The area of the sea here is over 60,000 miles. The depths exceed 9000 feet, that's going on two miles deep in some places. The explorer, Jacques Cousteau, named it the "Aquarium of the world" because it has over 5000 species of sea life. People come here from all over the world to fish, snorkel, scuba dive and every other activity you can name." Just then a school of dolphins broke the surface beside the research ship and started swimming playfully alongside. Spray from the waves felt cool in the oppressive heat on Brad's face. It smelled of the ocean and he liked that so he left it there.

After a few more miles north of their current position, the ship's motors were cut. Dr. Marshall said, "In this area we are going to do a density check for sea sponges and other sea-life in general. The pictures we take will be used to determined not only the types of coral, sponges and fish but with our sub and these cameras we can get to the sea bed, determine the stratum which could be made of sediment, flat rocks, stones or boulders. Then, with our HD digital cameras, we can quickly determine the species of each of these to the lowest taxonomic level and then track their growth and see how many are there the next time we come." "That sounds very interesting. Thank you for inviting me. My camera has some footage I don't want to risk damaging so I'll just pack that away and reload. I'll be ready when we get there," she said enthusiastically.

She was ready to go when the crew announced everything had been checked. Dr. England climbed in to start up the motors and Crystal climbed in beside him. After two minutes into the trip, Crystal was in total agreement with Jacques Cousteau, he was not kidding in his description. She was shocked at all the sea life here. There were massive schools of beautiful colorful reef fish and rays in the sparkling and sun lit blue sea. She even saw a couple of sea otters playfully swimming around the sub for a moment and then were gone.

As they approached the sea floor, the muddy sediment was what she first saw and then they approached a reef covered in colorful coral of all shapes and sizes, that's when Dr. England started Crystal's personal tutoring class. "We determine the densities of the corals as well as measure, as close as we can, the length and width of the Christmas Tree Coral for example. Our pictures are very important. Sometimes we use divers to get precise measurements but we measure the fish too, down to the nearest 5 cm." Crystal was impressed. She takes a lot of pictures but didn't realize how different angles and references make good estimates possible. She had never been to such a place and knew it would be a shame if the squid's population was allowed to get out of hand. The folks around here are settled in and they aren't going anywhere. This sea is their life.

Crystal tried to stay out of the way in the cramped sub as Dr. England was able to film for an hour without stopping. Some of the footage Crystal felt would be breathtakingly beautiful. She had also taken video as well as still shots. She knew it was crazy to do that because she only needed a few for her story but she wanted to show some of them to Brad and her thoughts lingered on him for a moment. "Are you ready to head back?" Dr. England asked Crystal. "Whenever you are?" She answered back. "Okay, here we go." He swung the small sub around and made their way back to the ship.

While Brad was laughing with the crew, enjoying some of Bud Martin's stories, Dr. Martin wouldn't let him out of his sight. Everyone he saw he would point to Brad and say, "This is the man who saved my life. Both, our lives, me and Rivera! This man right here, Mr. Brad Reno with his trusty wrench." Brad was getting a little embarrassed. A call came in from the university on Dr. England's phone. His assistant told Dr. Martin it was from their department and Dr. Martin called his office to see if there was anything he could do. His office administrator explained that a professor from Japan had called and wanted to talk to Dr. England and explained that it was important. She gave the name and number to Dr. Martin to pass on to Dr. England.

The RS-1 pulled up to the ship and the crew attached the cable. Crystal and then Dr. England disembarked and Brad was there to greet them. The crew began to hoist the sub out of the water. Crystal saw Brad, "Brad!" she called. "It was incredible. You have to do it, too!" "Wait just a minute. Dr. England has an urgent call to return," Brad said. "What is it?" Crystal asked. "I don't know." Dr. Martin walked around to where the two were standing. "How did you like that?" he addressed Crystal with a big smile. "Spectacular!" Crystal said, "I took a ton of pictures." "Good," he said. "I'm sorry for all the disruption earlier," Dr. Martin apologized. "I'm just glad you're okay," said Crystal. "Me too!" he seconded. Then he mentioned the school in Japan the call came from. It's where, the Tokai University Marine Schools are and they have world class programs with every phase of oceanographic study for both organic and inorganic studies. The president of the university, Dr. Kim Lee, has called to ask for help.

When Dr. England returned, he explained to the three what the call was about. It seems, Dr. Kim Lee, the President of Tokai University in Tokyo also has a squid problem. His, he said, is massive. A massive giant, what he believes may be the largest living colossal squid ever found has taken up residence in an area of Japan contaminated by radioactivity. It's the area contaminated after the earthquake and tsunami of 2011. He turned to Dr. Martin, "If you will take this assignment I will authorize, Ms. Brook and Mr. Reno to go along to assist. I am on the schedule to teach the rest of the week." Dr. Martin agreed to go.

Crystal made a quick call to her office. She tells her boss an abbreviated version of what just happened and of the call from Tokyo. She said, "I have another even bigger monster story. I'll send you what I have when we land and I'll even tell you what's coming next, but for now, I need two tickets to Tokyo for tomorrow."

Brad had the middle seat on the flight to Tokyo; Crystal had the window and Bud was on the aisle. The cloud cover was enough to block all but sporadic glimpses of the ocean as they soared west above them staying ahead of the sunset. The twelve-hour flight meant they would have to try to get some sleep on the plane. That wasn't easy for Brad, every little noise alerts him to wakefulness in public places.

After getting off the ground from LAX, Crystal looked over at him. His head was back against the headrest and his eyes were closed. "What's the matter?" Crystal asked, "You sleepy?" "Uh, no!" he flinched and looked up a little flummoxed. "You dozed off," she said. "Did not, just checking my messages." he said. "What?" she blurted out. "Never mind," he said. She loved his wit. "Have you ever heard of the "Devil's Triangle?" Dr. Martin asked Crystal. "I've heard of it. It's been compared to the Bermuda Triangle. You don't think giant squids could explain some of the disappearances there, do you?" she asked "Possible, but..." Bud answered. "Really? You think that?" Brad asked Crystal.

"I really just thought of it," she confessed. "I don't know what is or isn't possible with these things. It seems for something with no real means of propulsion other than short distances, they really get around."

After a few minutes longer, she looked at Brad again. His head was back and he was breathing deep and steady. She got as close to his seat as she could and rested her head on his shoulder. Unable to get comfortable, she raised up, gently, trying not to wake him, she took hold of his arm and pulled him over until he was leaning her way just a little so she would have her, Brad pillow, in a better spot. Then, she readjusted herself in her own seat to where she felt comfortable and there she settled in and began to relax. She yawned big and began to feel sleepy. Brad never let on that he was still awake but he smiled the slightest smile as he thought to himself. Awww, she yawned.

They landed at 6 am Tokyo time and the three-member team was greeted at the Tokyo airport by a young man dressed as an academic would dress in Boston with sport coat and bow-tie. Brad was impressed that he spoke English well enough to greet them in English, the sign he held read, "Dr. Martin". They were so distracted talking and looking around that they nearly walked past him. "I'm Bud Martin. You looking for me?" "Oh, Yes, Dr. Martin." Dr. Martin introduced him to Mr. Reno and Ms. Brook. Brad reached over and shook his hand. "Call me, Brad," he said. "I'm Crystal Brook, please call me Crystal." "I am Kaito, assistant to Dr. Kim Lee.

He explained that they would be meeting Dr. Lee at his office here in Tokyo. "If you can hold off a little while until we get to Dr. Lee's office for lunch, he may have made plans to go have a meal together sometime." "That's okay with me," Brad said. "I think it's a great idea. He'll know a good place to go." Crystal offered up. "Very true, Ms. Brook." Kaito replied in agreement.

They traveled in the compact car with Crystal's luggage in the trunk and Brad's in his lap from the airport into the city, toward Tokai University where they met Dr. Lee at his office. He stood quickly and walked their way with his hand extended to Dr. Martin. "It's so good to see you again, Bud." Dr. Lee said. "It's great to be here. I hope there is something we can do to help." Then he turned and introduced Crystal and Brad to their host. "This is Professor Kim Lee." Dr. Martin said. "It is my great pleasure to meet you both," as he reached out his smallish frail hand and smiled cordially. He started by saying, "We have an urgent need for someone with first hand, hands-on experience in dealing with a mammoth-sized colossal squid." He continued to hold Brad's hand in an effort to convey the importance of the matter. Mr. Lee was an older man and very proper when a serious topic needed to be discussed. His sharp emaciated features made him appear like an old soldier to Brad, reminiscent of WWII Japanese jungle war fighters. He was very friendly and frail but not soft. "So, thank you and Ms. Brook for making it here so expeditiously, Mr. Reno." he said with a strong accent. "I have read of your encounter with the colossal squid, you named him Wuss?" Dr. Lee's accent was strong. "That's right," Brad acknowledged, a little embarrassed he hadn't picked out a tougher sounding name for his 32-foot-long sea monster. Drago? After Rocky's Russian opponent, or Cujo of the Sea, maybe it's a girl, Ursula of course.

Dr. Lee continued, "Tokai University has an obvious interest in studying giant squids. I'm sure you understand the academic and scientific studies that may be advanced. You are world renowned for surviving an incredible battle with an incredible animal. I would not have wanted to be in your shoes, Mr. Reno." He turned to face Crystal, "And Ms. Brook, I know that you are the reporter that wrote the story. You have knowledge of these most unusual sea creatures?" he asked. Brad thought he sounded a lot like Sidney Toler from the old black and white Charlie Chan movies he loved as a kid. "Some recently acquired knowledge, thank you," she said. "Lately, I feel I am becoming too acquainted with them." Brad looked at her. She looked back without any expression. Dr. Lee acknowledged that he understood her wariness of these creatures, they are dangerous but he wanted the two of them to understand his perspective. "I see, Ms. Brook. You know, every time I see something from God's great ocean I've never seen before up close, I know I shouldn't be surprised but I just am. I'm even more astonished to be able to observe this magnificent creature. I sometimes just look up into the sky where I imagine God to be and just shake my head in wonder. There is scripture that I thought was ancient superstition that describes sea monsters like this in Leviticus, and he began to quote this passage from the Holy Bible, "Now, look what God has done, He has created a leviathian." and he went on. "Now, this is the moment in time when it is ready to come to the surface." "Yes," said Brad, remembering his old fisherman friend back in Charleston, "but in His great wisdom, He created an even bigger creature than that. He created the sperm whale, docile toward humans but finds nutrition not only in plankton, the smallest of sea life but the largest as well, the giant squid." Dr. Lee continued, "Yes, Mr. Reno, this is a biblical creature, not a myth or ancient legend and it's been hiding here all this time and growing. This one is ready to come to the surface but there are a couple of issues we must consider with this particular specimen."

Crystal pulled out her pen and pad. Brad looked directly at the professor. "This one has taken up residence in an area of radiation contamination from the nuclear accident I'm sure you're familiar with." "Yes, 2011," Crystal remembered the Fukushima Daiichi reactors damaged by an earthquake and subsequent tsunami. "That is correct, Ms. Brook," Dr. Lee acknowledged and continued, "One of our missions that we take very seriously in conjunction with our nuclear energy program is to monitor the contaminants regularly including radiation that is present on the ocean floor and absorbed by the plant and animal life populating these waters in the radius of the contaminated area. It seems we have a very unusual case, Mr. Reno. A mammoth-sized colossal squid has taken up residence in this area. We have no way of knowing how long she has been here. If we could get a bit of tissue, we could measure the level of radiation she has absorbed but other than that we do not know. We have surmised by her recent activity, that it appears she likes it here. The water is warmer, sea life is plentiful and she in no hurry to leave. This is a great problem and any help you might give us on how to deal with this creature as soon as possible would be greatly appreciated."

Brad was flabbergasted. He had never heard such a story. His first question to Dr. Lee was, "How do you know there's a mammoth giant squid where you say it is? Has anyone seen it recently? And how do you know he's still here and hasn't just moved on?" With a nervous smile, Dr. Lee nodded to give a second measure of assurance, "Oh, she's here Mr. Reno, we are certain of that. We managed to get a tracking device on her. We know exactly where she is and we are pretty certain she is the largest one ever recorded," as he continued to nod. Brad suddenly could see the concern on Dr. Lee's face and he had started wringing his hands together. Brad was, however, impressed that someone had gotten a tracking device on it. That will be helpful, he agreed.

"Dr. Lee?" Brad asked, "Is the one who put the tracking device on it the same witness who described it as a mammoth?" Dr. Lee replied. "No, Mr. Reno, he described it as the MOASM." Brad asked, "MOASM? What is that?" Dr. Lee replied, "It's an acronym and stands for, Mother of All Sea Monsters. He said when he saw it, fear inside crippled him." Then, what he said next nearly crippled Brad right there. "Mr. Reno, there is another reason he named it the, Mother of All Sea Monsters." Brad thought he knew what Dr. Lee was about to say. "Never mind the explanation. I get it." Crystal didn't yet. Brad completely understood the feelings of the eye witness, he had no problem with his reaction and thought that his was the most normal reaction he has seen, yet. "Did he give an estimate of its size?" Continuing to nod his head and affirming it with a smile, Dr. Lee answered, "Yes, the witness confirms what we have seen on radar. We have a creature here who we approximate to be 100-foot long. That is our estimate, Mr. Reno. There is another reason he named it the, Mother of All Sea Monsters." "Let me guess, Dr. Lee. She is pregnant." "Yes, very good Mr. Reno, she was but that was weeks ago. We never intervened and have allowed nature to run its course. We decided we would give her time to drift with the currents and back to the depths from where she came."

Crystal's mouth dropped open. She was left speechless. She needed to think about this now, to let it sink in. Wuss was 32 feet total and this one could be one hundred feet in total length that just gave birth to hundreds of baby MOASMs. He looked at Crystal, "If a 100-foot-long giant squid isn't the MOASM, then I hope I never meet it."

To Brad, MOASM sounded like a perfectly appropriate name, too, way better than Wuss. Well, it is more than three times bigger than Wuss. He turned to Dr. Martin, "What does laying around sucking in radiated waters and eating radiated food all day do to a 100-foot colossal squid, Doc?" "I don't know yet but it can't be good," Dr. Martin surmised. "Yeah, Crystal interjected, "it might have only been three feet long when it moved in here."

"Okay, Dr. Lee, how might we be of some assistance? Does the level of radiation we would be exposed to require protective gear?"Dr. Martin asked. "We will not be going into the contaminated area so you will not need any protective clothing," Dr. Lee assured him and went on to ask Brad a question, "Mr. Reno, when you faced Wuss, did you find any weakness in this animal?" Brad tried to recall, "Dr. Lee, the only the thing I could think of at the time was that his eye was so big and appeared to be the softest target for a harpoon. Keeping that in mind, a whale harpoon is the only way I would think to kill it quicker. If you want to knock it out and catch it, I suggest finding a whale sized tranquilizer that can be used on squids. Even small ones are difficult to manage in a net, it rarely ends well and I wouldn't recommend nets without tranquilizers. You will have to find a way to knock him out first if you want to move him to someplace else anyway. What I took away from my encounter with Wuss regarding his intelligence had to do more with his persistence in getting a meal. He did seem to recall where he got his last meal and he did seem pretty certain he'd find another one there. He may have seen me there the last time and remembered me. If his brain is as big and useful as his eyes, then I figure he probably knew what he was doing. He even made the same motions of sweeping the deck." That caught Dr. Lee's attention. He agreed, "Yes, it does seem to be able to linger against a current in an area as long as it wants to if it finds food there otherwise it definitely is capable of moving on." "Maybe that is only partially true," Brad stated questioningly. "What do you mean, Mr. Reno." Brad went on, "Wuss, we expect, may have traveled hundreds of miles to end up someplace where he nearly starved to death." "Interesting," Dr. Lee replied, "are you saying he went into an area he couldn't get out of?" "I'm saying there isn't much of a current where he wound up." Dr. Lee made a decision right then that Brad may have useful information that could help later and extended the invitation to them all. Turning back to Dr. Martin, he said, "Dr. Martin, I would be most grateful if you and your team would join us in this effort to solve this problem. Members of your team will have every resource available to you if you decide to become involved in some way."

Dr. Lee's phone began an unusual oriental song ring tone. He looked at it to see who was calling. It was his assistant. "Please excuse me." Crystal tapped Brad on the shoulder. He turned her way. "A hundred-foot mama squid just gave birth to hundreds!" she quietly expressed her astonishment. "I heard," he answered, "it may be too late to do anything useful."

When he finished the call, he came back to explain what had just happened. "There has been an accident at the entrance to the Port of Tokyo and the port has been temporarily closed by the Navy. All freighters have been rerouted to the Port of Yokohama until further notice. The reporting is that the propellers of a loaded freighter sank into a massive packed squad of squid up to 30 yards wide and 20 feet or more deep at the entrance of the bay. It was reported that upon striking the mass, the entire ship listed port-side causing several large containers to fall overboard forcing it to veer farther into a shallow area. Right now, the bow is stuck in sand and much of the freight may be in jeopardy." Dr. Lee looked at the both of them. "I'm afraid I have to cut our meeting short." "We are here, we may as well see what we can do to help," Crystal said. "Thank you. It is time for a team effort. Let's get down there," Dr. Lee said to Crystal. He called Kaito for transportation. Brad was asking himself; now why does she do that? Just pop right up and volunteer everybody. He wanted to ask her, so he followed them out the door.

"Kaito?" Dr. Lee gave instructions to the bow-tied young man who seemed eager be useful in any way. "Let's get to the Aqua-Line to Umihotaru Rest House. We will be closer and can get a good view of the accident from the 5th floor there." Then stopping for a moment, he considered Kaito's schedule, "Kaito? Would you be able to stay later today?" Kaito acknowledged with a big grin that he was available. "Please follow me," Dr. Lee instructed. They all turned as Kaito held the door open for them then ran ahead of them to get every door including the car doors. Dr. Lee appeared not to notice but Brad noticed, "Let's go Kaito!" he whispered to Crystal. "Oh, are you the Green Hornet, now?" she whispered back. He watched Kaito run in front of Dr. Lee to move a business office cart out of his path before Dr. Lee would have had to walk around it. It was a good thing because Brad noticed, Dr. Lee never looked up. Brad wondered how Dr. Lee managed not to walk out into traffic or something when Kaito wasn't with him. He squinted his eyes like Mr. Magoo.

In the car, Brad found out from Kaito, the Aqualine was a bridge-tunnel that crossed Tokyo Bay. Part of it was bridge and part of it was an underwater tunnel similar to the Chesapeake Bay Bridge Tunnel that connects Delaware to Virginia. The entrance to the tunnel was near the middle of Tokyo Bay with a five-story building there to provide a rest area for travelers. It contained a restaurant, souvenir shop and tourist viewing platform to allow a great place to view the entire beautifully colorful, brightly lit and very active Tokyo waterfront.

Dr. Lee brought a pair of binoculars and began looking toward the massive freighter no more than several hundred yards away listing at an even greater angle than earlier. A helicopter was circling overhead. From this point of view, he could see the freighter was slowly being moved as motion of the ocean underneath caused slow shifting sands to continue to give under the weight of the massive freighter and that caused the freight to continue to slide around. The scene was chaotic.

Dr. Lee moved his binoculars to see what was going

on at water level. He could see several smaller boats were helping crew members remove as much cargo as could be safely removed. At the rear of the freighter were several more boats including a tug and at least a dozen fishing boats. He could see a lot of activity by the men on the boats. Dr. Lee then contacted the local Navy Commander, Capt. Hanako, to offer his service. The commander reiterated how valuable of a resource he considered Dr. Lee and as things progressed, he would be available if Dr. Lee had information that could help. The commander stated he would keep him updated. Dr. Lee asked what the ships in the rear were doing. The commander stated that the repair team was unable to get into the water because of the aggressiveness of the squids. Local fishermen were helping by removing as many of the squids as they could but they have had their hands full with their aggressiveness.

Dr. Lee said he would also be available and ended the call. Crystal had taken some great pictures from this perspective but she wanted to get closer. "Can I borrow Kaito to take me around to see if I can get closer to see what they are doing?" He turned to Kaito, "Kaito, would you please assist Ms. Brook?" "Yes, Dr. Lee," then he gave a nod toward his mentor. "Thank you, Dr. Lee," she said and looked at Brad. "I can see fine from right here. Best view in the house." Brad explained. "For you maybe. I need some close-ups," Crystal stated. "I'll go," said Dr. Martin, "I'd like to get a look at what they are catching." "Okay," Crystal said and the three took off.

Dr. Lee talked with the commander again and

explained to Brad what he had learned, "As soon as the propeller buried itself in the mass it ground to a stop. The small pieces of squid carcasses had spread out and a feeding frenzy occurred. The mass became larger making it impossible for divers to get into the water to repair the propellers." "Where do you think that mass of squids came from? Is that common here," Brad asked. "Our fishermen do catch a tremendous number of squids here. The species of this squid hasn't been reported." Brad looked out toward the ship and said, "Whatever it is, it's native now."

Kaito followed an emergency vehicle and increased traffic to a side road that the rescue vehicles were using to reach the shoreline close to the ship. They made their way to a small dock where activity was hectic. A couple of news cameras were set up filming activity from the ground and a news helicopter circled overhead taking pictures. News affiliate's all agreed it was indeed a tense situation. People were yelling out toward the fishing boats while ambulance and emergency vehicles sat ominously close.

Crystal jumped out of the car with her camera and headed toward the dock where people were gathered. Many smaller boats had joined in the big haul around the larger ones to pull some of the squids from the waters.

As they hauled the squids in, the tenacious beasts would wrap their arms and tentacles around the nets and arms and legs of the fishermen in order to find their way back to the water forcing the fisherman to club the ones that were still alive trying to escape and stabbing others with homemade spears. The fishermen were yelling commands as well. She started taking pictures of the massive ship and the tugboat that was under great strain trying with unfathomable tenacity to keep it from digging deeper into the sandbar. Dr. Martin caught up with her, "Can you see anything from here?" He asked. "Not enough," she answered and looked up as a fishing boat was preparing to go back out for another run. Crystal jumped on board as it was shoving off. The fisherman was about to yell until she held up her camera to indicate she wanted to take pictures. Not happy about his uninvited guest, he decided he was not turning around, nodded his head and kept going while Kaito and Dr. Martin were left standing on the dock staring out at the waters. The fishing boat Crystal was in rounded the ship at the stern and what she saw there was shocking. She took a moment to compose herself, swallowed hard, held up her camera and began filming this massive horrific event. The fishermen were truly having to fight these squid to capture them and keep them in the boat. They would wrap tentacles around everything that touched them. Black ink splotches stained the waters.

Her boat captain pointed outside the perimeter established by the boats and lighting for the repairmen working on the propellers, she looked and saw an obvious shark fin. She looked around and saw more swimming close by. She never put her camera down while the fishermen kept working nonstop dragging these massive squids in tangled masses onto their decks and killing them there, piling them in a pile and going back for more.

After a while, Kaito decided he should go back to the others in case they needed him. Dr. Martin chose to stay with Crystal whom he had not seen since she hopped on the fishing boat. When Kaito got back to where he had left Dr. Lee and Brad, Brad asked him where Crystal and Dr. Martin were, he said, Dr. Martin wanted to stay. "What about Crystal?" He informed Brad that he wasn't able to ask her if she wanted to come back because wasn't there. That she had caught a ride on a fishing boat out to the rear of the ship to get a better camera angle. That made Brad immediately concerned and he asked him if he would take him to the dock where he left Crystal and Dr. Martin. "I would like to be there when she comes back," Brad said trying not to sound worried. Dr. Lee indicated it would be getting dark soon and wanted to come along as well. Kaito drove them to the dock.

When they got there, Brad found Dr. Martin but he said he still had not seen Crystal. She was at the stern where all the activity was going on. The boat that she had gone out on had come back but Crystal was not on it. The distance from the dock where he was standing, out to where Crystal was last seen was at least 300 feet away with a massive freighter in-between. From his perch on the dock, he couldn't see anything but the bow of the tall ship. As the day wore on, the tide began changing putting the freighter in more peril. It had sunk lower and as it began to lean, freight on board began to slide, occasionally one would tumble overboard creating fear and doubling the anxiety. The sun was getting low and lights began to come on. Among the brightest lights were those on some of the larger fishing boats. Dr. Lee explained how these lights actually attract squids to the surface at night. "The fishermen are going to make the best of this situation. More boats will be coming out soon." Brad began to think about MOASM. "Where is MOASM?" he asked. Dr. Lee had not thought about her until now. "She was in Fukushima last night," Dr. Lee stated. "How far is Fukushima from here." Brad asked. "About 300 kilometers." Brad's quick conversion in his head of .62 times 300 is about 180 miles. "That is a long way. There's a good chance these have nothing to do with her." Brad said to Dr. Lee, who put his binoculars down and started listening to what Brad was saying. "Do you think these might be the giant squid's chicks?" asked Dr. Lee. Brad had learned that was what you called baby squids. He was glad he took the time to read and learn a few things about these monsters. He felt like it gave him more gravitas, made him more believable when he was talking about giant sea monsters anyway. These were not babies but they may still be a long way from being fully grown. He also learned they were cephalopods, and that they were the most intelligent of all invertebrates. Dr. Lee had been available but so far, the locals have been taking care of this nasty business as fast as they can. Dr. Lee had been thinking of each problem as separate. It hadn't occurred to him before that they were related. "Brad, I need one of those squids." Brad walked over to a boat nearby with a load of squids in it and picked one out and brought it to Dr. Lee. He laid in on the deck and stretched out its tentacles. "It has eight arms and two longer tentacles. I'm afraid that I must confirm that there is a very high likelihood that these are from the genus: Mesonychoteuthis. I believe these are juvenile colossal squids." He turned the squid to look at the eye, "See how large this eye is? colossal squids have the largest eyes of all cephalopod." "Yes, I've seen them before," acknowledged Brad. "Yes, Mr. Reno, Wuss's eye must have been extraordinary." "Yes," he continued. "The size of the eye is important. It allows in more light since these creatures live in the deepest oceans where light is scarce, they are still able to see better than anything else down there." "Quite an advantage," Brad stated, "The only one who can see in a world of darkness." Dr. Lee turned over the dead arm in his hand and stretched it out. "You can see the suction cups all along the underside. Hundreds here of all sizes, I'd estimate the range of this one is 2- 4 up to 5 centimeters." The sun was going down. Brad looked at the repairmen working diligently to free the propeller from the tangled mass of squids and with the help of the fishermen, they were talking like things were looking up.

As it began to get later, more lights began to come on. "Did you say these lights attract squids?" asked Brad. "The small squid, yes," answered Dr. Lee. "What about the giants?" Brad asked. Dr. Lee saw the look of concern on his face. "Do you think they should maybe stop for the night?" "That would ensure a lot of people got a good night's sleep," Dr. Martin said. Dr. Lee sensed his unease and said, "I will contact the commander and relay to him, your concerns however these fishermen fish at night, every night. I do not think they will stop." "Can these giants track odors, like blood, in the water same as sharks? How does it keep up with its offspring?" Brad asked. "We do not know a lot conclusively about their behavior patterns," Dr. Lee added. "A lot of animals defend their young, don't they?" Asked Brad. "What are you suggesting Mr. Reno? That the MOASM could travel this far looking for her chicks?" "Is it possible?" Dr. Lee had to agree it was possible. "Then I do have a couple of suggestions," Brad said. "Check this squad for radioactivity. If they click, get the guy with the tranquilizer gun down here right now. We even have an expression where I'm from to describe this very situation. We would say it something like, get him down here, "not just now but RIGHT NOW" and don't let any of these young squids leave the area. As of now we have to assume until we can rule it out that these squids and everyone here may have been contaminated."

They decided to inform the ambulance attendees to get the word out they should make preparation for possible radioactivity decontamination for up to, he looked around, maybe fifty people. Dr. Lee did not hesitate to call Dr. Michu Chu from the marine science department. Dr. Chu is a fully certified veterinarian and she is the fastest to get things done. He called her on speed dial and after a brief talk he said goodbye. "She will be here as quick as she can with a Geiger counter." Brad nodded, feeling a little better. As the minutes passed, the stealthy darkness outside the brightly lit areas caused the watery landscape to gradually disappear. The darkness of the sky would only allow the brilliant lights of Tokyo to pollute its edges. Stars were becoming visible over the ocean.

Suddenly the silence was broken. A terrifying yelling came from a fishing boat that had dropped anchor. The anchor rope had been grabbed and jerked like a big fish taking bait and trying to get away. The boat was snatched hard and a crew member was ejected. The boat went mostly underwater and began to splinter apart. Two huge telephone pole sized tentacles arose from the dark waters. A lone voice broke through the quiet of the darkness, "Akkorokamui!" "Bakemono, Kaiju!

"What's he saying!" Brad yelled at Dr. Lee. "It's here!" Dr. Lee announced. Loud yelling in the background drowned out some of the words but the screaming was clearly understood by Brad. The tentacles crashed down on that fishing boat, overturning it and causing the fisherman to desperately swim for his life in a mass of squids but he immediately sank out of sight. The yelling of the boys and men in the background was all Brad needed to hear. Crystal was on one of those fishing boats and he had to go find her.

Left on the dock, Dr. Lee called Dr. Chu back as soon

as the attack began and she answered. "You have to hurry now; the monster is here." "The monster?" she asked. "The Mother of all Sea Monsters, MOASM is here! Prepare a tranquilizer dose for our new mother, she is probably over a ton. I would start there. See if you can get a shot from the helicopter." "I copy," Dr. Lee acknowledged, "I'll take care of it." He continued, "Go directly to the helicopter pad. I will have the pilot meet you there. Come directly here without delay. I'm having some things brought here with you from supply." Dr. Lee asked Kaito to call supply and make it clear there needs to be 50 body suits and a Geiger counter put in that helicopter before it leaves the ground. After Dr. Lee finished talking to Dr. Chu, he called Capt. Hanako to inform him of the situation and the plan that Dr. Chu would be on the helicopter looking for a shot to take with a tranquilizer gun. He explained how there was reason to believe that these were the offspring of MOASM and if so, she and the entire lot of squids were radioactive to some extent. He explained how Dr. Chu is also bringing protective garments and a Geiger counter to verify our suspicions.

Dr. Chu headed straight away without delay, she knew that this was an emergency and she was on the pad in minutes with her rifle and prepared dose of tranquilizer. The supply clerk was running as fast as he could carrying the coveralls and Geiger counter as the helicopter propellers started turning. He tossed them in and backed away as the pilot began to lift off and climbed as it headed toward Tokyo Bay.

CHAPTER 17

Brad ran to the end of the dock with Dr. Martin close behind. He saw a smaller boat with an outboard motor tied there to the pylon. He passed Kaito, who was helping the panicking people get out of the water. Brad turned his attention back to the waters where the fishermen were becoming confused and scared. What he saw was astonishing, a colossal squid stealthily attacking fishing boats. He could see parts of it as it would briefly come up from beneath the stern of the freighter and go back down. The waters were being thrashed; the entire sea was being made tumultuous by boats trying to get away. Debris and flotsam, began covering the waters. The bigger boats still afloat were heading out and away from danger while the smaller boats with their passengers clamored for the shore as some of them foundered.

Brad saw to his horror as one of the tentacles of MOASM, began rising up out of the muddy waters, displacing it as a tidal wave does, sucking water down to fill the void underneath as it was surfacing. "It's coming up!" somebody yelled. It was much larger than Wuss. Brad looked at Dr. Martin and from the end of the dock he saw Crystal briefly for the first time. She had climbed aboard another damaged fishing boat for better position for videoing. He was still a long way away and he knew she was in a precarious spot. At that moment, the end of a tentacle slammed down and hit the boat she was on knocking her down. Brad panicked, "We have to get over there!" His straightforward voice left no doubt in Dr. Martin's mind that he was going to be part of this rescue. Without any other words spoken the two jumped into the boat that was tied up there. Brad saw the boat Crystal was on was being pulled apart now and taking on water. She was up and climbing to the bow trying to reach another boat close by that was trying to get to her. Brad shrieked again as a tentacle swept that boat causing it to ram another boat suffering serious damage and stopping it completely. Dr. Martin heard the crash, looked up and saw what Brad saw, Crystal was stuck in a bad place. Dr. Martin fired up the 35 hp motor that made a sound that reminded Brad of Evinrude, the dragonfly from "The Rescuers" movie, he watched with his daughter years ago. Dr. Martin spun the bow around and gave the throttle a hard twist. The motor perked up and lunged forward. The bow rose up and the little vessel was on full bore and headed towards Crystal but the creature was still in the way.

"What are we going to use to distract her with?" the professor asked but Brad wasn't taking his eyes off

Crystal. "I don't know, just ram her I guess," Brad saw a paddle on the deck, he picked it up, looked around then took hold of one end and slammed the middle part of it down hard enough on the edge of the boat to break it in half. Half went off into the sea but he held on to his half. He figured that was as good as it was going to get. He then looked up toward the monster lurking mostly underwater now laying still. "Get as close as you can to that boat over there!" he pointed to the boat between them and the monster. "It's almost on top of her. I'll have a better chance!" "I see it!" Bud said, "okay!" "You get off on that when you can and wait for your chance, as soon as you do, I'll try to get back and get you," the professor said, "then we will have a better chance of getting away." Brad agreed, "that sounds like a good idea. We have to get close and you will have to get away fast. The one thing I remember for sure was that the eyeball is a large soft target and the only place I know where Wuss had a weakness for certain. The same may be true for his mother. If it doesn't kill her, maybe it will make her leave." "Eyeball, that makes sense," the professor concluded. "That's where I hit Wuss with the harpoon. It took a while but he did eventually die." Another wave swell gave Brad a good look at what they were going up against. The professor turned to Brad and said, "Do you think you're going to be able to get close enough to hit her in the eye?" "Let's get up behind the other boat and see if I can get aboard while she's focused on the lights. Get me close Doc, as close as possible." As they were closing in but still about 50 feet away Brad heard the professor yell, "Oh my God!" A quick glance and Brad saw what had upset him. The two of them watched the horrifying sight with their own eyes as a man was being dragged across his deck, still trying to hold on to parts of his boat up to the moment before he was jerked underwater. The entire animal recoiled around her victim. He was too far away to help. There was nothing anyone could do. The two tentacles could be seen snaking under water. Brad knew what was going to happen next. The creature was going to the bottom with her meal. "We have to go now," Brad yelled to the professor. "Give it all you've got towards the eye." Without question the professor aimed the small boat towards the monster that lingered momentarily just beneath the surface. He could see the eye there and it caused him to tense up because he knew what he was going into. Brad kept his eyes straight ahead and the professor had his orders and unless Brad said stop, he wasn't stopping. This man saved his life and he swore to himself that he would do whatever he could do to help him. He gave it all it had on the throttle, forcing Brad to sit as the bow rose up. Dr. Martin leaned over the edge a bit to look around the bow. He could see the humps in the water where the creature floated effortlessly and saw the monstrous eye near the surface. It was big as the window on his car. For the first time, the thought came to him that he might get the front of the boat stuck in there, right there inside the eye of this sea monster. That isn't something he wanted put on his tombstone as his epitaph. The professor also thought that there has to be some award for this kind of dedication to scientific research and academia. At the moment of impact, it seemed like the giant was looking right at them but didn't see them coming. Being preoccupied with its meal and not recognizing the little boat as a threat, it appeared not to be expecting any impact as if to say what crazy animal would attack me. Obviously, being treated this way was something it wasn't accustomed to. The monster's reflexes were instantaneous and it jerked violently, seemingly stunned, recoiled back from the impact and reflexively slammed the water with its huge tentacles, then went deep. The quickly made boat oar spear was no match for this animal. While the spear missed its target, it must have hurt a little to cause it to go underwater and the waters went quiet. Brad looked around at the carcasses of pink flesh-colored squids floating all around him, some still moving. The fishing boats had mostly backed off, the ones that could anyway, while several others were crushed and abandoned. They sat there waiting in anxious anticipation to see what was going to happen next. After a few seconds they both heard Crystal yell, "Brad!" The monster had moved, Dr. Martin suggested that it may be looking for a way out of this shallow area. He informed Brad that they had lost some of their control, the rudder was damaged and the gas was low so they needed a plan fast. Brad looked back, then, Dr. Martin added, "otherwise getting back to shore isn't going to be easy." He expected the freighter may also be unstable to move as well from its positioning and visible massive damage. It could roll over on its side. They could both see bulkhead and railing damage and damage to the structures from falling freight consisting mostly of train cars. He had to get to Crystal now while the MOASM was underwater. He lost sight of her again and the boat she was on. He gasped, "Where did she go?" He strained his eyes to see if he could see any blonde-haired passengers on the vessels close by but he still couldn't spot her in the darkness.

The professor was getting close to the side of the freighter. Brad yelled, "Get as close as you can to the ship, I'm getting out! You try to save the boat. If it starts to flood get to shore quickly but if you can save it, I'm sure it will come in handy!" Without question the professor brought the boat up alongside the freighter.

"Not like this boat is going to last much longer." Looking down Brad saw a foot of water in the bottom. "Get me up to that spot right there!" and he pointed with his finger in the direction he wanted Dr. Martin to steer. "I see a rope hanging! I'm going to try to use it to get on board!" Extreme necessity overruled extreme care when it came to getting close to this ship. Dr. Martin went ahead and bumped up against it and held it steady there in order for Brad to get to the rope. He tried to time the splash of the waves with his jump. Dr. Martin spun the wheel to ride the rhythmic wave but with the water splashing in his face and awkward jerking motions made it a challenge to hold her steady. When he looked up again, Brad was climbing the rope up to the deck of the freighter.

He made it to the deck of the ship, but when he got there, what he saw was stunning. The crew was running and yelling commands, trying to secure the sliding freight as the freighter continued to list more and more, ever so slowly, making it extremely dangerous for anyone on board or beside the vessel. These men were busy and seemed oblivious to what was going on below. Lights on the fishing boats were going out as MOASM, methodically invaded and overturned the abandoned boats.

He got to the stern and focused his eyes into the melee below. He yelled Crystal's name as he stared at the unbelievable sight off the stern of the ship not believing what he was seeing. There was Candy, standing there taking pictures of the massacre. At that moment he had a flashback. All of a sudden it wasn't Crystal standing there but Candy. There she stood, Candy, looking at this monster exactly the same way she did the night she was killed. Brad couldn't get the image out of his mind he had so clearly stored in the memories of his nightmares. He began to panic. In his nightmares he had never been able to save Candy. The incessant rocking and crash of colliding of two boats below the freighter startled him back to reality. There was Crystal with her camera poised snapping picture after picture of this monster's tentacles and the damage it was doing. She was no more than 40 feet away and easily within range of this monster. "Crystal!" Brad yelled. With all the noise and confusion, she couldn't hear him. The captain of the tug was in the control room yelling commands to his crew over the loudspeaker to use anything they could to defend the ship and pull survivors out of the waters, some with squids attached to their limbs and clothing. Crew members were using everything they could to flail at the creatures. From where he was standing, it appeared to Brad the tentacles were getting closer to Crystal but she wasn't looking in that direction, she was looking through her camera's viewfinder toward the fishing boats. Brad saw a rope hanging from the main mast of the fishing boat below where he was standing. He took hold of the rope he used to climb up and looked over and saw Dr. Martin hadn't gone anywhere. "You're a good man," Brad commended his bravery and climbed back down to his boat below. He saw the rippling waters between him and Crystal and knew it had to be the monster. Crystal was still out of hearing range with all the noise around and there was another boat about to collide with the one she was on. The monster was at the surface again and propelling itself to other areas, moving and stalking. A second helicopter was overhead and getting louder. "Crystal is over that way! She can't get off that boat!" he yelled to Dr. Martin. "We'll get her!" he yelled back.

On board the helicopter, Dr. Chu could see the tentacles and arms but the mantle would come and go out of sight. She saw two men and a woman as well and there was a danger that a stray shot could endanger them. She hesitated just as a tentacle wrapped around the chopper's landing gear and caused the pilot to panic. The copter sat down hard in the water. Brad saw it just before it hit the water, shrieked and leaped into action. "Get us over there! Quick!" Dr. Martin was already in motion. Brad dove into the water the last few feet where the boat was unable to maneuver through all the debris and swam up to the helicopter's door. Dr. Chu was sitting and stunned and the pilot was working to get out. The rifle hadn't been fired so Brad held up the gun and looked at Dr. Chu for approval. She nodded in the affirmative. He went to the door of the chopper and scanned the immediate area. He didn't see MOASM anywhere. He shouldered the rifle and checked on the two passengers again. Dr. Martin managed to get to the door with his small boat and began to haul them out. After they were boarding his boat, Brad grabbed the protective garments, "The PPE's! And here's a Geiger counter," he said, and switched the Geiger counter on. It immediately started clicking. He threw the PPE's along with the Geiger counter into the boat. "Here's our confirmation!" he yelled to Dr. Martin, "Take these two and this stuff over to Dr. Lee, they look a little shook up, I'm going back to the freighter," Dr. Martin nodded he understood. "When you get finished with this, come find me." He began climbing back up on the freighter. He had a much better view from there. The men on the freighter working to secure freight were fighting a losing battle. He scanned with a sniper's stare, several fishing boats, looking for Crystal as they were continuously being tossed around making it difficult to see anyone on them, then he began looking at others that had foundered or capsized until he finally spotted her. She was holding onto the railing of the boat she was on and was trying to lift her camera up to take pictures with one hand like she was invisible to the monster or something. "What is wrong with her?" he asked himself. He could see her but he couldn't get to her. He looked around and saw the fisherman lying unconscious beside the control room but Crystal hadn't noticed.

Brad saw a rope that he could use to climb down from this side. He looked down to the water and saw a wrecked boat being held against the side of the freighter by the current. He slid down the rope and landed in the boat. Another wreck was a few feet away. Brad used the masthead rope and swung across the water to the other boat. When he did, he nearly lost his grip from shock when he realized how close he came to smacking into one of MOASM's rising tentacles, he could have kicked the thing. The boat he was on and the one Crystal was on was only about 30 feet away but both were unable to move other than drift or be pushed. Brad couldn't reach her, but she could hear him from where she was standing.

He yelled at her and she heard him enough to look up. She was only slightly startled when she saw him. "Where you been?" She asked. "You're missing all the action!" "Lookout!" He yelled, as he watched a tentacle climb up the side of the boat right where she was standing. He saw that the rope he had just grabbed hold to for balance reached to the head of the mast that was now tilted in the direction of the boat that Crystal was on. He unshouldered his weapon and held it like a pistol with his left hand, stretched out the rope slack and got a good grip with his right hand, leaned back and took a running leap off the side of his boat toward where Crystal stood. He aimed the rifle directly at the mantle of the monster as he was swinging over her. The same moment he found his target and pulled the trigger a tentacle swung his way and slapped the rifle out of his hand. He kicked at it but missed just as the shot caused her to flinch. He landed directly behind Crystal and she grabbed his arm to steady his landing as he quickly looked back at the MOASM in the water. He could see the tranquilizer dart fully imbedded in her mantle and although he caught Crystal off guard, she had to admit that it was very nice to see him. "See, I knew I picked the right man for the job. You almost missed the excitement," Crystal reported. "Oh?" He asked. "Hold on!" and he swung the two of them back across the water to the boat he had been on. As they passed over the beast she looked down and saw the giant pink-bodied squid was fighting the anesthetic to stay awake and was moving around, just below the surface. When they got to the other boat, Crystal raised her camera and started snapping pictures again. He looked down to what she was taking pictures of and saw the pink-bodied giant lying motionless in the remains of hundreds of her babies. Brad looked at the staring eye and felt like he could see that there was intelligence there to some extent.

A crew of the closest surviving fishing boat began

moving in to help position his boat to capture this magnificent animal. Brad ran over to the railing and yelled, "Net! Net!" He tried to play a little charades with his hands until the fisherman finally caught on. Brad saw the two men's heads nodding as they moved towards their net. Another crew moved closer to give them a hand while Brad began searching for a rope to tie around the monster. A loud bang coming from the deck of the freighter made everyone look up. A huge train car tumbled over the side landing on the port side of the ship with a huge crash creating even more turbulence in the waters. They wanted to get out from under this giant mouse trap.

The men quickly attached the net to the wench of the largest fishing boat around to lift the still squid out of the water. Many smaller ones were nearby but they were focused on this one right now. The professional fishermen began to gently haul in their catch like they did every night. The creature was unconscious for the moment with one tentacle literally draped around a boat rail. Another boat made its way beyond the creature and around to deliver their rope to waiting crew members on the other side to be secured. Every effort was being made not to kill but to capture MOASM so scientists could learn from it but that was secondary to the need to remove it from this area due to its proximity to people. When they were about 2/3 of the way around the monster, she took a random swat using the tentacle from the boat and slammed it into the top of the net pushing it down. The jerk was tremendous and stopped their momentum entirely. "We're in trouble if she gets tangled up in this net before they get her out of water. Give it all you got," yelled one of the captains. The weight of the giant was incredible and the wench strained under the resistance.

Suddenly the creature sensed something was wrong as she started to waken and began to stir. The initial bump was hard but the experienced fishermen continued to reel in and cinch up the net. She slowly began moving a tentacle, following the rope and methodically untangling herself, slowly becoming free from the fishing net.

"Do you think we can get her out of the water?" Brad asked Dr. Martin. Brad waved to the crew to try to lift her up. Brad looked at Dr. Martin and Crystal and said, "I'm getting out here! Keep in touch and keep your other eye on the net!" "Okay, Brad good luck." "You too, Doc." Brad exited the boat and climbed on board the closest fishing boat and began to assist the men working the net. MOASM was so huge, it made you think it couldn't possibly be real, then it would move. Brad couldn't believe how huge MOASM was, at least three times larger than Wuss. Shivers went down his arms and his neck hair stood up just thinking about how large it was. It overwhelmed his senses such that he could hardly stand close to it. It had suction cups bigger than his head. He saw another skeptical fisherman shaking feverishly trying to get more lines on the monster and securing the net before it's ripped apart. He froze for an instant when he saw Crystal had gotten closer. She was only about 10 yards back with her camera in her hand. He called to her, "They are trying to secure her now." All the tentacles were below the surface with the net closing in over her ready to start lifting her out of the water when one of the crewmen yelled, "Stop!" The wench was beginning to creak and the wench arm was close to collapsing. The boat was listing.

The veterinarian was too careful not to overdose the rare creature and now she was beginning to awaken. Every man on the water here was trying to quickly get this giant tied down. Crystal thought of the water version of, "Gulliver's Travels".

Brad was in position with the others attempting to keep her within the net with the tentacles and arms tied down as the crew figured out what to do. Suddenly, she pulled one of her tentacles out of the confines of the net with the ease of someone getting up from a chair. Crystal started taking pictures so measurement estimates could quickly be made. She felt more confident now having recently watched how the scientists on the, "Think Tank" takes pictures at angles to capture different points of reference. It turned out MOASM was bigger than expected and quite a bit of her was still hanging out of the too small netting. She was semi-conscious now and every few seconds she tried to move. They were only able to close the net partially from this angle. The estimate of the giant's mantle length was no less than 50 feet and her tentacles, several feet longer than her eight arms, could reach upwards of 50 to 60 more feet. Anxiety was high on the boat and Brad was ready to pitch in along with the bravest fishermen there to help keep this beast enclosed in this net. These men standing here, at the ready, holding tight to his section of netting are not new to this game, most have been fishermen a long time and have seen creatures, as the Bible says, "great and small" taken from the sea but the beast they call MOASM, the fishermen all believe to be the Mother of all Sea Monsters and have the utmost respect for her. They could see suction cups larger than their heads with razor sharp jagged teeth circling each suction cup. As the beast was being hauled closer to the side of the boat a distinctive jerk was felt from the net, then another and another.

The fishermen tried again to use the wench. The strain on the motor increased as the net slowly eased out of the water. What everyone saw then was astounding. Squids on top of squids were clinging to the side of the net. There were various sizes small and even some pretty large ones had attached themselves there, perhaps a hundred or more. All of a sudden, the motor of the crane was no longer able to pull the net up. The captain stopped the hot motor before it died. The quiet came suddenly and for a moment stillness was in the air but the men felt a change in the normal movement of the ship under their feet. This movement felt like the ship was starting to list. Every man looked at each other wondering what they were going to do next. One of the crewmen yelled in Japanese, "You have to empty out the net it's going to pull us over." Another yelled in English, "The beast is going to capsize the ship!" Brad looked at Dr. Martin and Crystal with the shrug of the shoulders and casually said, "I didn't know they would do that." Dr. Martin responded without looking up, "You learn something new every day." "Do you think we should cut the line?" Crystal asked. Brad knew what Crystal was saying. They had to let the beast go or risk the ship and more lives. They could all feel the ship listing and was afraid capsize was inevitable and soon now. Brad looked at Dr. Martin and said, "Dr. Lee is not going to be happy" "Don't worry, Brad, I'm sure he'll get another chance." The ship was taking on water before they finally managed to cut loose the line. The entire crew watched under the lights as the ship recoiled and the bundle quietly sank back to the ocean floor from where it came.

As MOASM escaped into the deep part of the channel, the fishermen knew that they had missed their chance. Everyone watched in still silence as the monster disappeared. After a few moments the fishermen turned back to their work. They were each given PPE's and told where to take the squids and where to go for decontamination. The fishermen were familiar with this procedure, after all, this is Japan.

There were still plenty of smaller ones feeding on the mass of squid tentacle tips and mangled mantles left behind so they turned their attention to what remained. A couple of surviving fishing boats worked together to continue sweeping the areas with their nets. Many smaller scavenger fish had invaded the area and were added in because of their exposure as well. Brad thought the sharks behaved like the buzzards back home, milling around watching everything until it's their turn.

Crystal took her last picture of the last moment of the monster slipping her gargantuan body almost elegantly and effortlessly out of the unsecured portion of the net and slowly faded into the darkness. It will go on to make the cover of National Geographic Magazine and the amount of video and still photos she took while risking injury to life and limb turned out to be more than enough for more than one documentary. A Pulitzer for this story, we'll have to see, if she can just learn to elaborate a little bit on her story, Brad said jokingly to her over coffee.

Crystal took a moment to stop and turned to Brad, "By the way, you rescue a girl in a pretty impressive way." She had a little smile on her face but Brad didn't see it that way. He nearly lost her the same way he lost Candy. A wave of melancholia swept his thoughts as he tried to disguise the tear in his eye with a little smile of his own in answer to her eyes. "I'm starting to think that's the way you do things, Brad Reno." "Yes, panic-stricken, like Courage, the Cowardly Dog," he answered back. "Who?" she asked. "Didn't you watch cartoons as a kid?" he asked. "Sure, I did, I was a Power Puff Girl." Brad looked at her and smiled. "I can see that. I liked them too," he said. She smiled back because she knew what was inside this man. His self-deprecating manner didn't hide the fact that he saved lives today even if she and a handful of others were the only ones who knew it.

Bud brought his boat up to where Brad and Crystal could get back in and took them to the little dock where Dr. Lee and Kaito were busy helping at the decontamination area.

Brad and Crystal walked over to where Dr. Lee was standing with Dr. Chu and her pilot. They were okay, just shook up. Brad looked at the two of them and asked, "Do you speak English?" "Some," Dr. Chu answered. "You were very brave to do what you did out there," Brad said. "Thank you," she answered. He turned and shook the pilot's hand. "Good job!" he offered. The pilot shook his hand and nodded that he understood.

"Dr. Lee, I know you are disappointed in the way things turned out today," Brad consoled him. "I am only disappointed in the lives lost and damage done, Mr. Reno. As far as our new mother goes, perhaps she will find a home in some deep part of the ocean and live a long life without future interference from man." "We can only hope," Crystal added. "Yes," Dr. Lee opined further, "The land has its carnivores and the sea has hers, magnificent, but now we know, the Mother of all Sea Monsters is the Leviathan," he said in true warrior fashion. "In the meantime, we have our work cut out here to clean this area up and get Tokyo harbor back opened." Then they all stood there reflecting on the day for a moment. "We learned one more important thing, Mr. Reno," Dr. Lee added and Brad looked at him. "If we are ever in this position again, we will use a higher dose of tranquilizer." They all agreed on that.

Dr. Lee then invited the three to a discussion on hydro-agriculture the next morning by a professional on the subject. Dr. Martin was anxious to accept. Brad said he would pass on the lecture but would be very happy if he could recommend a great place for dinner for them.

"I feel like I haven't eaten in a couple of days," Crystal said. "Okay, my treat," offered Brad. "Would you like a nice big steak or maybe a platter of sushi?" "Yes, let's go with the sushi and calamari. That's all I've been thinking about all day," Crystal chided back and everyone laughed, "and a nice white wine of course...", they all stopped simultaneously and said, "Not!" in unison. Tonight, it's steak for me," Crystal said, as she was getting her decontamination bath. "I've heard they have good beef here," came Brad's voice from another curtained makeshift shower beside hers. "Some say Kobe beef is the best in the world!" came Bud's voice from the end stall." "I'll be the judge of that," Brad said. "Me too!" came from Crystal. Then they all walked out, showered, wearing new PPE's and headed to the hotel.

Later that evening, their taxi pulled up to the beautiful Teppanyaki Shima Restaurant with traditional Japanese architectural and the setting was beautifully decorated with foliage and arrangements from local flower shops. The three enjoyed a fabulous meal. The oyster appetizer was superb. The bread with oyster soup was delicious together but the Kobe beef rib-eye aroma from the table beside theirs made Brad's mouth water. "I'm having that," he motioned to Crystal. "Smells wonderful," I'll have one as well. Let's get some wine," she added. "Of, course, my dear," and reached for the wine menu. He found a regional Syrah he thought sounded interesting and Crystal approved.

Following the waiter carrying steaks, still sizzling on the platter, to a table next to theirs, the aroma wafting through the air, a single solitary fly lands on Brad's plate. He waved the fly away and said to Crystal, "Do you see that brazen little devil?" Then he said to the fly as it continued flying around, "Leave and don't come back. I'm watching you, and don't worry I know you are out there. Don't think I've forgotten." "What was that about?" Bud asked slightly confused. "Nothing, just that it's either coincidence or I seem to attract the one thing that shouldn't be where it is," Brad explained. "I don't think it's you," Crystal assured him, "It's no coincidence that most species of animals and insects can find hospitable environments over nearly all but the most extreme places on this planet," Crystal asserted. "That's what bothers me," Brad said, "the ocean has to be the same way." They all agreed on that.

The waiter worked doubly hard in describing their dinners in English. He talked about how the beef came from the Tajima breed of cattle and how Wagyu describes a well-marbled or streaked with fat, piece of beef that results in tender, melt-in-your-mouth, flavorful steak that can be prepared, however you would like it.

The meals were mouth-watering delicious and the

steaks were tender and aromatic. Brad agreed, his was close to steak perfection. It compared well to what he could do on his grill back home. Crystal decided she was going to be the judge of that contest. After dinner they made it to the airport hotel. Crystal had talked to her boss and he needed her back right away with story in hand. She booked their flights back for the next morning. Later that evening, Brad walked Crystal to her room. They had to be at the airport early so she told him she would knock on his door when she was ready to go. Then she kissed him softly on the lips, gave him a very nice hug and said, "Goodnight, Brad Reno," smiled at him and softly closed her door.

On the plane ride home, the TV mounted on the wall up front started showing the news. It was totally being spoken in Japanese with English subtitles so Brad hadn't been paying any attention to it. Suddenly a cheer went up in the cabin and folks around him were all looking at him with big grins. He looked at the TV and there he was the moment he was swinging across the deck of the ship to reach Crystal, rifle in hand, making the shot. A big, "Yay!" came from the cabin. Everyone was watching when MOASM knocked the rifle out of his hand. When he landed beside Crystal on the boat, the crowd in the cabin cheered again, "Yay!" The entire moment was captured on video. There was even a slow-motion version with a stop action photo where it can be clearly seen that the end of one of the sea monster's tentacles had wrapped around Crystal's leg. A close up of Brad's face showed something most people never see, the look of a man charging headlong into danger with no doubt in his mind about what he was up against and no certainty of how it was going to turn out. His look wasn't fear though, he was studying the movements of the creature, looking for his chance. He remembered thinking that he didn't need much time. It was just like swinging across the creeks and gullies as a kid, except this time he was swinging over a colossal squid and with that in mind he was waiting for his opening to go. His plan was to swing over there and take the shot with the tranquilizer, grab Crystal and get away safely again. To his audience, his action showed a total disregard with the consequences to himself while his, "All for one and one for all" mentality was clearly apparent and everyone on the plane could tell that it took an enormous amount of bravery as well as an enormous effort to do this. They witnessed a man defiant against a sea monster, no different than fables of knights battling dragons with swords drawn and without an instant of hesitation as to what he had to do, he did it. His, "I'm not taking no for an answer," attitude and immediate swing into action to help free his friend out of the slimy creature's grasp and then to swing back with her out of harm's way, that's when the cabin passengers yelled again, "Yay!" His actions seemed a very American thing to do by the passengers on board. One gentleman sitting near him got his attention and said excitedly, "You look like, Rambo!"

For a moment there was total silence and the passengers on this plane learned something important. They learned why heroes who come out alive after risking everything don't like to talk about it. All they want to do is fall down on their knees crying in thankful gratitude to God that they have survived. Brad realized at that moment why we needed Hollywood heroes. It a way to show real heroes what we think of them.

The flight attendant made an announcement over the intercom so that everyone on board knew that Brad Reno and the woman he rescued, Crystal Brook, were on board so conversations among passengers in the cabin picked up and several people came up to shake Crystal and Brad's hand, smiling big and being extremely polite, saying things like, "I just had to meet you," and "You are so lucky, Ms. Brook that Mr. Reno was close by." She didn't tell anyone that he was her, "protector," but she did say kiddingly, "That's his job," and looked at Brad with a sheepish grin. Now, they are for the moment, the country's newest celebrities. The handshaking didn't stop until they had left the plane with about everyone's hand being shaken. "You're famous, Brad Reno, in Japan!" Crystal said, and they both laughed as they headed to baggage claim. Brad carried his bag.

They arrived back from Japan at the airport in Charleston and at Brad's apartment after 4 am. He opened the door to his apartment for Crystal to go in first, he followed and kicked the door closed with his foot and let out a sigh. After slinging his one bag on the floor of his living room he looked at Crystal. "I'll put this stuff away later." She looked at the pathetic little bag that had maybe three dirty things in it and smiled. She liked his sense of humor; he was funny when he wanted to be. "Want a glass of wine?" he asked. She answered without delay, "Sure, I'd love a glass. Something dry?" "That's exactly what I have right here." He smiled and held up a bottle of wine he pulled out of his small wine rack under the island table in his kitchen, grabbed his handy corkscrew and opened it with skilled dexterity and expertly poured two glasses of this pleasant red table-wine he found at Barboursville Vineyards, a winery in Virginia, after a wine tasting on a trip to DC. He handed Crystal her glass while she was checking messages. "Hmm," she said as she took a sip. "This is really good. What's it called?" "They named it Octagon," Brad answered. "I love it," she said and then turned back to her messages and found she had an urgent one waiting for her from her boss. She called him up and Brad overheard enough of the conversation to know that she had to be back at her office this morning.

Brad watched her as she took notes and was suddenly saddened by the thought of her leaving. He took his glass and walked out onto his deck and stood there looking out over the saw-grass marshlands of the low country, the home of the low country boil and some of the best crab-cakes you can possibly make. He tells friends that they easily rate as high as Maryland's famous crab-cakes which he also loves. He stood there watched the seagulls flying in the near darkness and a great white heron on the bank with his attention focused on the task of looking for something to move in the mud under the security lights in front of his pencil thin toes. He noticed lights from a shrimp boat heading out for a morning of shrimping about 200 yards away as a no-see-um bit his arm. He slapped it just as Crystal opened the sliding glass door and joined him on the deck. "What are you doing?" She asked. "Just enjoying the view," he answered. Crystal stood beside him and looked out across the saw-grass as it waved in an ocean breeze like fields of wheat in the mid-west. "It's beautiful here," she said, Brad didn't say anything. After a few seconds Crystal reached out her hand and laid it on top of his as it was resting on the railing. "I have to be leaving soon," she said. "I have to be back at the office in the morning and no way I'm going to make it if I don't leave right now." Brad turned towards her and tried to hide his disappointment. He wanted her to stay. He had developed such a closeness that he wanted to show her around here. He wanted to take her to dinner at his favorite local restaurant. He also knew that he was going to miss her. She said, "I just got off the phone and can catch a flight out at about 7:00." Brad looked at his watch and saw it was closing in on six now so he knew she had to be going soon or she wouldn't make her flight. "Oh my goodness, are you going to be able to make it?" he asked. "I'm going to try," she said with a halfhearted smile on her face. "Can I help you with anything?" Brad asked. "Nope, I think I'm all set," she said as she stepped toward Brad looked him directly in his eyes and said, "Brad, I can't tell you how amazing this week has been. I wish I didn't have to run off but I want you to know that I think you are an amazing man and thank you for saving my life." She reached up, held his cheeks in her hands, leaned forward and kissed him gently on the lips. He stood there in total surprise by her very sincere kiss. As she leaned back away from him, he focused in on her eyes and not being able to think of anything else to say, all that came out was, "You're welcome," with a big smile swelling up he couldn't hold back. She returned it with a big smile of her own, leaned forward again and gave him a big hug around the neck and an extra kiss on the cheek. "Walk me to my car," she said. She held his hand and pulled him along with her knowing she was going to miss him too. She could feel an emptiness in her chest as they walked along together toward her car. "I'll be in touch with you as soon as I get back and get started putting this story together." "Okay," Brad said.

Opining further, she added, "It was funny the way those two monsters came up about the same time on opposite sides of the world after succeeding in being hidden for so long. We were at the right place at the right time." "If you say so," Brad chimed in. She stopped at her car and turned around one last time before getting in. "Thank you again, Brad," she opened her car door and got in. Brad touched her hand on the door frame and then gently closed the door. He heard her car start, said good-bye one last time and with a little wave and smile, he turned and began walking away. He glanced back one last time. She was sitting in the driveway on her phone with her brake lights on. Then, Brad saw her backup lights come on and she started backing up, she turned around and speedily drove back to Brad. She already had her window down. "New assignment!" She called out the window. "Just got a call from Marshall England. He thinks they may have found another giant and they want us to come right away." Brad stood there looking at her, not entirely sure he didn't just hear her say, "Martians have just landed in England, and they want us to come right away," he couldn't believe what she was saying. She picked up her telephone to cancel her ticket reservation taking her back to her office in St. Petersburg, FL and asked about tickets to Los Angeles the next morning. She hesitated before making the reservation and looked up at Brad. "Is 11 a.m. good for you?" she asked Brad. Before he could even think of a rebuttal, he had no other answer ready except, "I guess so." Crystal let out a laugh when she saw his mouth had dropped open a little. She reached out and took hold of his hand and mouthed the words, "Thank you," to him and went back to her phone to complete the reservations. She finished texting in her information and got confirmation in her email and hung up the phone. "All ready!" she said and stared at Brad for a couple of seconds. "You hungry?" He asked her. Crystal got out of her car, walked up to Brad and reached out her hand to intertwine with his arm. "Starved!" she assured him. He held onto her arm, led her around as they turned in unison to head in the direction of his car. "I know this great little place not far from here," he stated.

"Oh, you do, do you?" Crystal asked playfully. "Yes, they make the best crab-cakes for breakfast this side of Maryland," Brad assured her. "I definitely should try those," she said. "You should," Brad agreed, "What about coffee?" she asked knowing she was about hear a Brad Reno coffee critique and couldn't help but smile at him. He quickly took the bait. "Coffee?" he asked back in an incredulous tone. "Ms. Crystal Brook, you are in for a real treat, and I say that knowing full well you have a true appreciation for fine coffee." "I do," she added. "We can take my car," he offered and they both turned to go that way. He went on, "Just wait until I open the door for you," he explained. "Oh, you're going to open the door for me?" she asked. "I will, as I was saying, just wait until you walk through that door. That robust aroma will lift you off the ground," he concluded.

He gestured artistically upwards with both hands and said, "You are going to think coffee was invented here. You might even forget what you came here for." And for the first time since she met him, he smiled a genuine smile at her, she was sure of it. "The ahhh," she started, "the crab-cakes, Mr. Reno?" "Yes...the crab-cakes are delicious," exclaimed Brad. "I definitely need to have some of that, too," she said smiling.

Brad was right again. As they were finishing up, Crystal looked up at him, "I must say, Mr. Brad Reno, you are a fine judge of crab-cakes and....." "And?" Brad asked. "And the coffee, hot and smelled wonderful.

It hit the spot." "I thought you might like it," Brad said. Then with a side look and a slight grin she decided she wanted to tease him a little while they enjoyed more of the steaming coffee.

"So, Rambo, are you going to tell me you were afraid, again?" There was a pause and a deep crease furrowed his brow. He turned to look at Crystal and in his most serious voice, explained. "I was. Seriously Crystal, when I saw the danger you were in I was frightened to death." "Couldn't have proved it by me," Crystal deduced, "as a matter of fact I think you've turned into quite the adventurer, Mr. Brad Reno. We make a good team, don't we?" "What?" he asked, "No, I was afraid!" "Nope," she said, "I'm certain you weren't." "But I was, really I was!" he exclaimed. "Nope, I don't believe you!" she held her ground.

The End

www.ingramcontent.com/pod-product-compliance
Lightning Source LLC
Chambersburg PA
CBHW060928190726
48286CB00002B/675